Daguerreotype Dreams

And Other Stories . . .

Daguerreotype Dreams

And Other Stories . . .

14 Dark Tales of the Civil War

Volume One

By Mark Stattelman

Copyright © 2004, 2007, 2019
by Mark Stattelman

All rights reserved.

ISBN-13: 9781702154468

Dedication:

I am forever beholden to those intrepid souls who took time out of their busy schedules way back when to read and critique the first six to ten stories I ever wrote:

Kirche, and Matt (wherever you are today), Paul, and Jerome. My heartfelt Thanks guys.

And to Sharon, who, as a teenager (back in '93-'94), and I'm guessing out of simple curiosity, picked up the completed and printed first draft of the first novel I ever wrote and read it, beginning to end. I'm in awe of her to this day for having the stamina to make it through. That Eighty-four-thousand-word abomination (okay, maybe it wasn't that bad. It was a labor of love after all. But it was pretty bad) will never again see the light of day if I can help it. Except to meet the shredder blades, though the shredder will probably spit it back out. Thanks for reading it all the same. Like I said, I'm in Awe!

Table of Contents

Dedication: v
Note to Reader: ix
Preface... xiii
The Trap..1
Sabre In the Road 13
The Homecoming 19
No Greater Love.. 27
The Burial 37
The Owl Tells a Tale... 49
Just Plain Bad Luck 69
The Bugler..91
House of Unspeakable Things 103
A Blind Eye, a Missing Appendage, and a Friendly Card Game!..125
Only Those Most Deserving............................145
Daguerreotype Dreams..................................... 161
A Challenge 175
Of Mice and Men 201

Note to Reader:

If you happen to notice some of the same characters appearing repeatedly in these stories, and in volumes two and three, it is because they are from a novel that I intend to eventually publish. I just have to rein it in from its current five hundred plus pages. As a matter of fact, the story The Trap is directly from the novel (though it was a short story first, and though in the first person here and the third person in the novel). Most of the scenes these characters appear in in these stories, however, are original content—so no spoilers (other than the aforementioned story The Trap). I just love playing with the characters. These characters include Ms. DuBarry, Morris and Esther Garvin, Jemilayah (a.k.a. Jem), Minnie, Miss Nell, etc.

Along with the other titles in the Dark Tales of the Civil War Series,

Volume Two: I Fear Only the Dogs

Volume Three: And You Shall Not Live

Volume Four: (as of yet untitled)

Be on the lookout for the novella, The Dancing Man.

All coming soon!

Preface

On June 2, 1955 my Appalachian grandmother turned one hundred. She was still extremely lucid in thought and speech, even though she wasn't ambulatory in any sense of the word. It was just previous to her birthday that she shared her small secret with me. Due to her lucidity, and her utmost veracity, as she was not a teller of tales by any means, I tend to believe her.

It was in the late winter of 1864, and she and her older brother, Frank (who passed away prior to my birth, and for whom I am named.) were playing one clear, bitterly crisp morning. The chores completed; the children decided to explore along the edge of the frozen river. Frank walked out onto the icy surface first, just to make sure it was still frozen enough for them to skate upon. He then went back and retrieved her. Having been poor, their skates were makeshift, of course, and the blades often broke and had to be re-filed, or replaced. They took turns and thoroughly enjoyed the quiet of the early morning. The birds chirped. As the sun began its ascent, the ice hung sparkling from the low hanging branches on the snow-covered riverbank. If you listened closely, you could hear the lower branches, which were laden with ice, actually scrape the frosty ice-covered river when the wind blew. The effect was hypnotic. The other kids hadn't yet made it out of their respective houses, so the two had the large and open expanse of the river's surface to themselves. It was on a glorious spin, instigated by Frank, that her blade snapped and sent her sliding awkwardly across the ice. The snapping of the blade had forced her foot the wrong way, and she broke her ankle. Frank had to go for help.

As she lay in immense pain, waiting for his return, she was becoming cold and numb, her tears freezing upon her cheeks. To take her mind off the pain, she began to rub a spot into the ice next to her bundled head and face. She tried to hum a tune while she worked on the ice, but her thick scarf muffled the sounds and stole her breath. She pulled it down and continued working on rubbing the ice. Her face was close to the surface. Her warm breath touched the ice, melting the top layer of it ever so gently before steaming up and disappearing into the grand expanse of Virginia sky above her. Gradually, a dark shape took form beneath the layer of ice next to her face: A watery image, at first only a darkened blur, a cloth-wrapped form. A face appeared, the nose tapping only once against the bottom layer of ice. An eye looked up at her from a watery grave. It was a peaceful eye, open wide, still frightening for an eight-year-old girl. And yes, the darkened spots were clothing, the dark blue cloth of a uniform, a Union soldier. She could see his face clearly, preserved perfectly in his frozen death. It all happened quickly, only seconds. She screamed and rolled away, closing her eyes in terror. When nothing more happened, no cracking open of the ice, or evil mist of death rising up to enfold her and pull her down, she rolled back and looked again. There was only the soft, slowly moving current beneath the thinly melted surface of ice, just a small window on the world below.

When Frank returned with her father, she told him. Of course, he didn't believe her. They bundled her up and lifted her gently onto a sled. Several people had gathered now and they didn't mention it to the adults, but a few of the boys got together and searched for the body. They started with the thinning ice patch she had looked through, nothing. They broke it open. The ice was about an inch thick around its edges, the water moving steadily beneath it, bitter cold where it splashed up into their faces when they tried to peer through. They moved farther down the river, hoping for a thin spot to break open, also hoping that the body had gotten snagged on something, perhaps turned and wedged on rocks in the riverbed. Luck was not with them. They never found the body and after several hours they gave up looking. Frank and the other boys decided she was probably lying. She swore that she hadn't lied, and Frank wanted to believe her. He knew she wasn't one to make up tales, at least not unless it was part of a game and all sides knew that it was such. Yet they had to give up the search. By spring they had forgotten about it, and no one farther downriver ever sent news of finding an extra Union body, perfectly preserved in form and feature.

I cannot tell you, dear reader, how many sleepless nights that Union soldier has caused me. How he came to be there is widely open to question and speculation, as well as how he met his demise. The most intriguing question for me, however, is how he came to be at that particular moment in time, at that particular spot, looking up through that particularly clear icy patch of window at that particular little girl. Was it simply to scare the bejesus out of her? My grandmother promised me that she would ask him when she reached the other side. This, of course, was our little secret. Generous soul that she was, she was undecided in her heart about heaven and hell, and couldn't see sending fellow human beings into eternal condemnation. She simply called it the other side. I guess I'll have to wait my turn before finding out. Though that truly would be a hell if this question never gets answered in all of eternity. But I guess it wouldn't bother most people. It would be like asking why the sun rose in the east and set in the west.

And so, while other children would play with toys of this world, I would drag this soldier out of my imagination and dress him in all sorts of adventure. I would make up wild stories as to how he came to be where he was then. That is how I was led to the following stories, only one or two of which pertain to this soldier. Please enjoy.

Frank Larchmont, Feb. 23, 1983

Frank has since passed on, but I, rest assured, dear reader, am carrying on his act of writing stories. I won't confess as to which stories are of Frank's own hand, and which are of mine. All I say is read and enjoy!

M. S. 2004

The Trap

Carl Higby's death wasn't suicide, and everyone knew it. Overseers don't kill themselves. They simply don't; It isn't in their nature. Tying it to Lee's surrender was almost laughable. Not only was it a fact that news of the surrender reached us only after Higby's death, it wouldn't have mattered in any event. The truth would have mattered though; It would have sent a wave of terror rippling out for miles around. As it was, the truth was there, an undercurrent of horror, which everyone tried to ignore. It jangled the nerves like a sudden gust of wind jangling chimes about on a dark hot summer night. The chimes of truth had much stronger reverberations, and were far more chilling, especially for me, for I was the spring that sprung the trap, the mechanism of his demise.

I had seen the overseer only twice up close since I had been on the farm. He was a short, stocky, powerfully built man with a perpetual scowl. He had one large shock of gray-brown hair in the middle of his head. It sat high and back from his broad forehead. This one shock of hair was surrounded by a moat of baldness, and surrounding that was a strip of hair running from one side, round the back of his head to the other side. He had one eye which appeared smaller than the other, or perhaps it only appeared so from years of squinting his face in a scowl. To say that he might not have been such a bad person given other circumstances, perhaps in another time and place, would have been a fallacy. His job required a hardness. I need not describe this hardness further except to say that he reveled in it.

My first encounter with him was one morning early upon my arrival. That is to say, one of the first few days I was able to move about on my own, having been carted to the house from a nearby ravine

The Trap

where I had wandered and stumbled, after having been left for dead by my brothers in arms. He had stepped up on the lower step leading up to the verandah, where I was sitting taking in the morning air. This was before I had taken up the habit of going fishing with Mossy, a small slave boy whose only job seemed to be feeding the chickens in the morning. As it was, at that time I could only be up and about for short periods.

So, there stood Higby. He had some business to confer with Miss Nell about, though I wasn't quite sure what it could be, at least until I remembered that the judge was away on business, which left his twenty-four-year old daughter to run the place. He seemed uncomfortable around the house, as though he didn't dare enter, especially when the judge was away. He was a man who knew his place. He wore a leather vest, over a shirt that seemed a little too fancy for him. He had a pistol tucked into his belt, and wore high leather riding boots. He wasn't sure how to take me, and I don't think he liked my intrusion. He definitely didn't seem to like my being in the house. He didn't say anything at first.

Minnie, a slave girl of about fourteen had seen him coming and had run in to get Miss Nell. I could hear her stuttering, trying to relay that he was here. She stuttered when trying to speak regardless of the information she was imparting.

Higby nodded to me, almost grudgingly, and then looked up into the sky. It was as though he was going to mention the weather, but then decided he didn't have to converse with me on any subject. I was the intruder after all.

"Yes, Carl?" Miss Nell appeared, pushing through the door with one hand while holding a fistful of skirt with the other, keeping it from dragging the porch. Her hair had a premature gray streak running through it, only on the left side, which was the side exposed to me at the time. She had it pulled back in a bun, not tightly, and a strand of it straggled loose, hanging across her cheek. Her eyes were weary and sunken, dark crevices forming underneath. The war, sacrifice, uncertainty. She would have looked attractive in easier times, and still did, her body comporting a weary voluptuousness.

The mulatto house slave, Jemilayah, who was very near in age to Miss Nell, though much less ravaged by worry, was beating a rug a short distance away on the far side of the verandah. Minnie had been helping her to hold it, at least until Higby appeared and she dropped her end to run get Miss Nell. Jemilayah didn't show any expression change whatsoever, and merely kept trying to shake it out herself. Minnie soon exited the house behind Miss Nell, and went back over to help. Higby ignored them, but appeared ill at ease around Miss Nell.

Miss Nell waited patiently for him to respond.

He looked everywhere except at her. He would look only fleetingly at her before glancing over to where I sat. "Well, Ma'am," he started. He looked at me a couple more times, his larger eye glaring.

"Carl Higby, meet Captain Elias Stark," Nell said matter-of-factly.

Higby nodded at me again, grudgingly, trying only minimally to hide his aversion.

"Captain Stark will be staying with us while he recuperates." She paused, looking at Higby.

He cleared his throat and tried again: "Well Ma'am, I need money to pay Finley for the shackles, and also for a bag of grain . . . The horses . . ." He was almost squirming, hating my presence, my observing that he had to grovel.

"Of course." And then again, more to herself as she went into the house. "Of course, you do."

Higby looked a little more relieved. He glanced over at me, and then spit tobacco juice off to his right. He scraped some mud off his boot onto the bottom step and glanced over at Jemilayah, not consciously, I don't think. It was more of an unconscious action, though on the surface, it could have been taken for a challenge. Jemilayah didn't act as though she noticed him one way or another.

She moved gracefully, and was very similar in build to Miss Nell. She wore a muslin dress, and wasn't unattractive. She bent and gathered the rugs to take them inside. Higby watched her, absently. Minnie, though trying to help Jemilayah, kept faltering with her end of the rugs as she looked at the overseer with not a little trepidation. He ignored her. He looked at me again, and then spit another large chunk of tobacco juice into the dust. The two slaves carried the rugs into the house, and Nell returned right after they went in, not quite long enough for Higby to work up another scowl, or another spit for that matter.

The second time I saw him, several days later, his demeanor was less accommodating:

"Leave her alone," I said, not raising my voice. The element of surprise being on my side.

Carl Higby stopped his grunting exertions almost immediately, but didn't turn around right away. Only slowly did he turn, hatred creeping across his features, overshadowing the embarrassment he should have felt. A horse whinnied and knocked its hoof against the side of the stall as it shifted. The lantern hung from a nail, high enough so that the light shone down at an angle, leaving half of Higby's face in darkness. His lips curled in a snarl as he turned. His pants rested around his ankles, exposing his buttocks.

Minnie looked back over her shoulder, a multitude of indescribable expressions washing over her face. When Higby dismounted and turned to face me, she was completely exposed, her hips high, glistening in the flickering light. She immediately fell to the ground and reached for her garments, making guttural whimpering sounds as she tried to cover herself. She then held the clothing bunched in front of her as she lay curled on the barn floor, covering and uncovering her eyes in spasmodic movements. Unsure, her mouth working furiously, nothing but garbled sounds starting and dying before ever taking form in the night air.

Higby took a second to gain control of his temper, slowly pulling up his pants, anger luminous in his eyes. He took two steps toward me as I pulled the hammer back on the revolver, the chambers rotating. His pupils grew large with hate, his smaller eye squinting into a twitch. Involuntarily he glanced to where his gun had lain on the stack of bundled hay. The whip was also gone. Both items now in my possession. The only thing left was an almost completely empty whiskey bottle. Slowly, a malicious grin formed on his lips. "You won't shoot."

In a flash, just as the hammer clicked back, Minnie ran wailing past my elbow and out through the barn door, disappearing into the night.

"Why not?" I asked, watching him for any signs he might move. "I've killed better men."

The Trap

His smile waned, while his derisive glare remained fixed on me. The horse's tail swished against the stall door. He shifted again. Another horse whinnied and moved restlessly about, snorting and nodding.

I shifted slightly on my crutch, hoping to relieve the pressure on my leg. I was unsuccessful in the attempt. The discomfort not only remained, but grew more intense.

"Soldier boy, you're makin' a big mistake comin' 'tween me and a slave girl. You got no business interferin'."

It was my turn to glare. "Maybe," I said.

I stared at him. "I've never owned a slave. I reckon I don't know the proper treatment of them, but seeing as how she is the judge's property, thereby following that she also belongs to Miss Nell, and I don't think she would be too pleased to hear of your actions. . ."

He started again in my direction, then stopped when I took a tighter grip on the revolver.

"Tell you what I'm gonna do," I said. "I'm gonna move on out the door now, and I'll leave your piece in a place where you'll be sure to find it in the morning. And your whip."

He started again, making like he was going to lunge. He was drunk, but not wholly stupid, in spite of how things appeared. I only had to shift the gun a bit to remind him of its existence.

I moved outside, watching him the whole time. I shut the barn door and barred it. I figured he would sleep it off and come for his reckoning another time. I would have to keep an eye out. He would have been able to climb up into the loft and out the upper door on the other side of the barn if he was so inclined, provided he wasn't too drunk. I might have to sit up part of the night. I expected him to lay low for now, but there wasn't any way to tell for sure about any man. I went slowly on up to the house. I sat on the verandah a little while and enjoyed a smoke. There seemed to be no stirring from the barn. Eventually, I moved on in the house and went to bed. My wounded leg kept me from sleeping too soundly, at least until the early morning hours.

In the morning, the news spread quickly of how Higby was found swinging from the rafters, a

The Trap

hangman's noose around his neck. One horse was loose in the barn. This, it was said was the one he had drunkenly stood upon to hang himself. No one questioned the absence of his whip and gun, two things he always kept close at hand. Also, no mention was made of his hands being tied behind his back.

They must have been hiding in the stalls and beneath the hay, quiet as mice, waiting. . . Like many a night before, I would imagine, they waited for the opportunity. Never before had they been able to get close enough. Never before had things fallen so easily into place. I was the well-oiled spring, the mechanism that sprung the trap. The mice had caught the cat and they all then disappeared into the night, as quietly as they had come.

Often, I awake in the middle of the night, his face before me, filled with terror. I hear the sound of the wooden bar clapping into place to lock the barn door. How it now sounds so much like the hangman's gallows to me. I see him drop. Often times I can faintly hear him scratching, clawing at the inside of the barn doors, his larger eye aglow with horror as they approach in smooth unison, no sense of remorse showing on their faces. I can hear him mewling in my dream; But I know this is not true. He was a hard man, though not a good one. He would have fought for his life. I feel no sorrow for him, not really.

In essence, it is not the truth I fear, but the avoidance of truth. This causes me to wake up in the middle of the night in a cold sweat. For I can hear it rumbling beneath the surface, like a freight train heading for an unknown destination.

Sabre In the Road

After becoming separated from my regiment, I tried to find them. I rode for several hours, searching in vain. Soon I came to a fork in the road. I wasn't sure which way to take. It was then I noticed a sabre, standing upright directly at the middle of where the fork split, its blade stuck deep into the mud. I rode up to it and looked around. Not seeing anyone, I dismounted. No sooner had my fingers touched the hilt when a shot rang out, ricocheting off the handle with a loud ping and then a thud as the lead buried itself in the mud. I stood still. The sabre sang and quivered, but remained stuck upright. "Don't touch that," came a voice from behind me. The quivering tapered off and silence ensued.

Keeping my hands in the air, I looked back over my shoulder. Still I didn't see anyone, at least not right away. Then I noticed movement. A horse standing behind some trees over my left shoulder, a fine looking roan, was calmly eating grass. I turned slowly, searching the wood, straining to move only my eyes. I saw only the woods. Perspiration ran from my forehead, rolled down the side of my nose and down my neck. A fly landed on my cheek, moved, and then buzzed away. I could smell the leather of my saddle as my horse shifted behind me and swished his tail. I searched the trees again. A squirrel jumped from one tree to another, scuffling to maintain his hold on the second branch. Lower down in the tree the squirrel had vacated, I saw him. A good ways above eye level, in a tree closer to the road than the one the horse stood near, was a Union soldier. He was actually standing on a thick branch, revolver in hand, looking down at me, grinning. The midday sun shone from high above and behind him, leaving his face in shadow except for his lower jaw, his teeth showing between curled lips.

"Get back on your horse."

I moved slowly, doing as asked. I was contemplating my chances of going for my own revolver. He seemed to read me. "Don't do it." a voice said. I wasn't sure whether it was him, or my own thoughts.

Once in the saddle again, I felt almost confident enough that I could dodge a bullet in the back. Almost. I pulled back on the reins and my horse reared a little, its weight distributed to the haunches, the right front hoof pawing the air just above the road. The horse's head turned left, under the tight hold of the reins. His eye rolled back, as if trying to read me. Letting my hold on the reins loosen, he calmed down. I started him to the left, slowly. We only got a few steps along.

"Not that way!" Came the voice.

I ignored him, still moving slowly. He shot me. My horse reared at the noise, whirling around completely, climbing at the air. I came close to falling. "Gall damn, you! You shot me."

"I warned you."

I looked down at the blood trickling from my arm. He had nicked me. This yank was a damned good shot. I thought twice about trying to run.

"You go that way and I'll fill you full of holes."

"You best get to shootin' then," I said, waiting.

He didn't respond, other than a short laugh. I didn't move. He had the upper hand. He seemed far too jovial. It bothered me. Having the gun out made things easier for him.

I shook my head and moved over to where the road forked right. "You haven't seen the last of me Yank!"

"I reckon not, Reb," he responded casually.

I rode on, fully intending to circle back at some point.

It was an hour or so later that I was standing in the road, my horse trying to drink muddy water out of a rut left by a wagon wheel. I lifted the reins. I felt groggy, tired, as if in a dream. Horses approached at a fast gallop. It was Jared Little, and Todd Greenly, two men from my regiment. They were out of breath with excitement, flustered and disheveled, their horses frothing at the mouth. "We ran into a contingent of Unions," Todd said, trying to catch his breath.

"Wiped out the whole regiment," said Jared. "We barely made it out of there." He wiped his sleeve across his nose, still trying to catch his breath.

"Lucky you came this way." They were both still panting heavily.

"Did you see a sabre stuck in the ground back at the fork?" I asked.

The two men looked at each other blankly, then at me. Each of the two shaking his head.

"Or a Yank in . . ." I started, looking down at my arm. There was no blood, not even a slight nick, and I decided it best not to pursue it. I tugged upward on the reins and pulled my horse's nose up out of the puddle.

We rode quietly on together for a good hour or so. The afternoon was hot and uneventful. We didn't run across any of the enemy the whole rest of the way. Finally, just before dusk, we came up on another small contingent of our own fellows. I calmly chewed on a piece of straw while I pulled the saddle from my horse. He looked around at me. "I sure wish you could speak," I mumbled. "Cause I ain't completely sure about things, events from this mornin'. . ." He didn't respond.

The Homecoming

The fog was just starting to lift. I had been walking for hours, searching. The rumblings were dying. The battle was growing weary of itself it seemed. Bodies were lying haphazardly, one across another all about the field, at least as far as I could see. Others were searching, wandering, trying to wake companions, both Union and Confederate. I shook one young boy that I recognized. Eyes wide, he didn't respond to my shakings. I glanced down at his hands, his fingers laced with his own intestines. I moved on, finding another one I recognized, then another, and still another. It was confusing. Everyone I had been in battle with was dead. They were all dead. But they couldn't be. I saw others, some I couldn't quite recognize, and others who seemed only vaguely familiar. There was a cannon at one spot, an area that men had been dug in pretty well, firmly grounded. Fighting had been fierce. The artillery men were also lying about, cold to the touch. One man, Jack Strather, a fine fellow, was draped across the top of the cannon barrel, one arm hanging down, and the other missing completely. Impossible, I thought. Could it really have been this bad? Could we have lost everyone? No, of course not. I looked around.

Two men were coming in my direction, carrying a wounded man on a stretcher. I spoke to one of them. He ignored me and they kept on moving. I grabbed the other one's sleeve and tugged at it. They stopped momentarily.

"Excuse me," I started. "Have you seen . . .?" The second man adjusted his grip and they moved on, ignoring my exhortations, only momentarily glancing in my direction. When they had gone a little further, the second bearer looked back over his shoulder, puzzled, but again, just a fleeting glance.

I happened to see another two men, again carrying a third man. This man I recognized. "Harry!" Thank God. Harry grinned at me as best he could. I was suddenly struck dumb. He was in pain, which was understandable as the lower half of his body was missing. "Stuart," he said weakly. He seemed delirious with pain. I watched them carry him off. I then spotted Captain Curry.

I waved my arms frantically, hollering at him, tripping over bodies as I went. A hand reached out and grabbed my ankle. I went down, face forward into a muddy quagmire. I raised my head, and wiped the mud from my cheek. I looked down at the man whose chest I used to push myself up. He didn't mind, never would again. There was blood on my hands, I reached up and felt the side of my head, a wound, dried; the blood was from my friend lying on the ground.

I untangled my trouser leg from the hilt of someone's sabre. I had dragged it from his hand. I didn't bother to replace it. This man wouldn't care either, not anymore.

I looked around for the Captain, and there he was riding off, waving his sabre high above his head, stopping momentarily as his horse maneuvered the sea of death beneath its feet, then spurring his horse forward again. He glanced back, his face fixed in determination, a smile of courage, the horse rearing, its legs rising high in the air, a vision of glory. He'll get a medal, and a promotion, I thought. I'll fight another day with him, happy he is on my side. Onward he charged.

It was then I saw the girl, no more than four or five years of age, on the edge of the battlefield. As I proceeded to make my way over toward her, I passed more and more men. Battle raging still in this section of the field, men were falling, joining comrades left and right. All about them men were squirming, writhing, dying. While this fighting raged, still more men searched, turning bodies over, looking for friends, calmly diligent, composed and oblivious. Lead was flying, the sound of it whipping through the air. Though I had heard these sounds many times before, still they seemed strange, almost

The Homecoming

completely alien and ineffectual. One explosion, followed by another, then the sound of grapeshot pattering the ground about me. Still I moved on, wearily. More shots ringing out, mingling with men's cries, while smoke whirled round my head, swirling, made me dizzy. I couldn't see the girl, then she appeared, still there, rubbing her eyes, crying.

She wore a small white dress and tiny black shoes which were somewhat scuffed. Blond curls surrounded her face, which appeared cherubic in form, mild in nature. Her visage was aglow, her cheeks red from crying. Her eyes were a watery blue and shone brightly. She rubbed her right eye with one hand while holding tightly to a tiny doll with the other.

"Now, now," I said, in what I hoped was a soothing voice while the sounds of battle raged behind me. "You shouldn't be here. This is no place for a pretty young thing to be." I decided she couldn't live too far away, though how or why she wandered off I could not answer. Her parents were probably hiding in the cellar of some nearby farmhouse, either unaware of her absence, or frantic with fear upon the realization that she was missing. She looked at the ground beyond me. I turned and saw a man's face looking up from the ground, death upon his features, too horrific for the sight of a little girl. "C'mon now," I said, gathering her into my arms. She still looked at the man. I carried her away from the sight, to the edge of a copse of trees. There was a road just beyond it. Setting her down, I wiped a tear from her cheek. She looked at me, no longer crying. "Such a beautiful little lady," I said, tousling her hair. "Now, which way is your home? She pointed in a direction and off we went. She grew more lighthearted with every step. "Your parents will be very happy to see you," I encouraged. She smiled up at me, grasping my hand a little tighter, pulling me onward.

Eventually we came to a small farmhouse and she grew very happy again. The place looked familiar, and I remembered marching past it a few weeks back. We went into the small yard. It wasn't much of a place. She kept pulling me. I noticed the deserted look of the yard. And as she pulled me past the side of the house, I took note of the boarded windows. Ah, there it is, I thought, the cellar door. It rose up

The Homecoming

out of a hilly patch of ground, a short distance from the house. I expected her mother to come bursting out at any moment, frantic, yet overcome with joy at her appearance. But she pulled me past the cellar. There was a small garden just beyond, at least, it had been one once. A little picket fence surrounded a squared off area, much overgrown. The fence was no longer white, and it was broken in places. She let go of my hand and opened the tiny gate.

"Want to see my flower?" She asked, much delighted to be home.

"Why certainly," I responded, very happy for her, yet wondering about her parents, where they might be, knowing they would be worried. I glanced over at the house again. It was disturbing. What could have happened to them? Could they have been taken away? Certainly, they wouldn't have left her intentionally.

"Here it is," she pointed gleefully, falling to her knees before it. It was beautiful, solitary, blooming brightly in the sunshine. It tilted toward the sun, its petals open wide, white, lightly tinged with pink, an orange-yellow center. The flower appeared full of life, swaying in a light breeze, opened as though smiling up at the bright blue sky, leaning out away from the narrow edge of a headstone. I remembered it well, the day it was carved. I looked back at the little girl now, trembling, suddenly recognizing my own daughter. I broke down. She had been dead since just before the start of the war. And my wife soon followed. She was pointing at the second headstone now, my wife's. "And look," she said cheerily, pointing at a third.

"M-me?" I asked, choking on my tears.

"Of course, silly!" She giggled. "Who else?"

I sobbed completely then, overcome with a tremendous relief.

No Greater Love

Celia waits patiently for the letters. At the beginning of the war they were more frequent. She looked forward to them, adored them; languished when they did not come for long periods. She would cry. Heartbroken, in the grip of tremendous depression. Then one would arrive. The clouds would part, and her heart would soar. It has been months now though. Is he dead? Has he merely forgotten her? Found another?

Celia had met Albert at a social event, a ball, before the war. He was a Yankee, but she didn't mind.

He didn't play the games that the others often played. He expressed his love for her right away. She would sit thinking of him while she combed her hair. I am beautiful, she would think. And he had told her that. "The most beautiful girl in the world" he had said. He kissed her passionately. No one had ever done that before. It was indescribable the way he made her feel. Frustrated, she could never put it into words. She had tried several times to start a diary, never able to make it work.

The war came too fast. They had only known one another three short months. Albert implored her to wed him. She loved him dearly, and wanted to, but her folks forbade it. Her mother and father were tried and true southerners. Her father saw the seriousness of the affair and wouldn't allow Albert to see her anymore. She would sneak out after dark to meet him in the woods. The first one or two times they met she held him at bay. They would kiss, but that was all. The third time was different. Frustrated, Albert told her he had signed up for the war and was leaving within the week, to fight on the Union side, of course. She became angry. How could he leave her? He made stronger advances. Their kissing was more heated. A fiery hot passion arose within her. Celia was not the same girl she had been. Perhaps it was the moon, or the stars, or some other strong pull or push. Perhaps it was because Albert was due to leave soon. What if he never came back? They had been lying on the floor of a clearing, surrounded by the darkened woods. The leaves and pine needles formed a soft bed beneath them. The night air was warm. A cool breeze would occasionally blow, pushing a loose bit of hair across her cheek. Albert kissed her again, moving his hand beneath her clothing. She was hesitant at first, pulling his hand away. They kissed. He tried again. Again, she brushed his hand aside. He became angry with her; told her she didn't love him. She swore to him she did. He pulled away and she followed him. He came to her again. This time their lips met, their bodies merged and the night swallowed them whole.

On her way back to the house that night she stopped and looked up at the large willow tree. Oh, how beautiful it looked to her in the moonlight; how beautiful the whole world seemed. Reaching up she grasped its frothy, drooping leaves. She spread the willow across her cheek and looked up to the moon. God, what beauty. A cool breeze swept across her face.

As she crossed the yard that night, she thought about climbing into the porch swing and falling asleep in the night's sweet embrace. But it was late. So instead, she floated up the front steps and climbed straight in through the parlor window. Suddenly, a shot rang out. Her father shot her.

Why she had chosen to climb in the window instead of using the front door is unclear, perhaps she was working under the assumption that the window was more romantic, or perhaps the door squeaked. In any case her father could have shot her just as easily in the doorway, and probably would have dropped her cold. As it was, she was bending over to bring her following leg in when he fired.

In the clear light of things, he would have come to see that it wasn't all bad, for he had only taken off her left earlobe with the volley. There was a tremendous amount of blood and commotion, of course, and he thought he had killed her. He reloaded immediately, and shot himself in the head, missing his own earlobe completely, but causing greater damage in the main.

Eventually, Celia recovered, though still missing her earlobe and her father, though naturally not to the same degree. Her mother never did get over the shock of her father's death, however, and continued to blame Celia. She fell into the habit of drinking, and was soon bringing home all sorts of strange men and women. One of these men, the worst of the lot, she married, much to Celia's chagrin.

Celia was in the meantime receiving letter upon letter from Albert. He expressed his love, and she sent letters to him expressing hers. They would get together at the end of the war, he promised. Until then, letters would have to do. For Celia and her mother lived in the heart of the Confederacy, just south of Richmond.

Celia's mother, having married a man, let him run the house. Unfortunately, he felt he had property rights to Celia also. She was quick to disavow him of this illusion, as best she could. He still chased her round the house, every time her mother passed out with drink. She swore she was going to kill him

Soon the money was gone, and they had to take in boarders to survive. This was a relief. Celia wouldn't have to be alone with her stepfather. She tried hard not to be. Still he groped, and she slapped and fought as best she could. He never got further than grabbing her here and there at odd times when no one was watching. Still, she only had Albert's letters to console her. She would sit for hours, pouring over them. Often times they were slow in coming, due to one circumstance or another brought on by the war. But in all, brothers on both sides, families, broken and split in varying areas of the country, no one was really sure what mail was Union mail and what was Confederate mail. In the end, however, the Union tried to stop supplies, and mail from reaching the Richmond area and they were pretty much successful. Some letters managed to find their way to her.

Celia's mother soon passed on, due to the bottle, poverty, and general heartbreak.

Her stepfather, no longer being such, due to her mother's death, begged and pleaded to stay on. Celia relented out of sheer pity. She still hated him, but on behalf of her mother, she consented. Soon, however, he was back to his old habits, and a boarder finally told her what she should do to get rid of him. The old lady told her a story about how a slave girl ridded herself of a mean and cruel master. I don't think the old lady realized the importance her story was given in Celia's mind. But Celia took it to heart and used the sound advice:

She served her ex-stepfather his meal one evening, with a special treat. She had spent time crushing a glass candleholder into very fine fragments, and mixed it in a pleasant tasting hollandaise sauce, his favorite. It was only a short time before he was bleeding internally, as the intestines do not function well with glass working through them, however fine it might be. Soon he was dead.
The old lady who had given her the advice, refused to eat another bite in that house and moved out almost immediately. Celia, herself, was surprised at how cruel, though effective, this method was. The old woman never went to the authorities for fear of being tried as an accomplice, and probably never mentioned the story about the slave girl to anyone

ever again either. And of course, the local militia was busy with other things, even if they had been apprised of the situation, which they were not.

There was only a problem of what to do with the body.

She tried burying him in the backyard one night, but a dog kept following her about and digging him up.

She finally settled on a good lye bath. She then picked the rest of the meat off the bones, and fed the local pack of wild dogs a little more each day until all of it was gone. Of course, then she had a problem with wild dogs coming round expecting to be fed on a daily basis and she couldn't afford it. She thought about taking in boarders again, not as dog food, of course, but so she could bring in some money to support herself.

She soon found a lady who had a good racket going with a group of girls sewing canvas tents together for the army. The lady also sewed for the Union army, having no qualms about where her money came from, though she had to smuggle the material out to them. This suited Celia just fine as she felt she was helping Albert out in some way. The war would soon be over, she hoped, and all sins would be forgiven.

The skeleton, oh yes. Celia had shoved it in an upstairs closet and forgotten about it. One fine rainy afternoon, she pulled the bones out and tied tiny strips of canvas to them to hold them together. It was a project, but it worked.

And now she drags him out and waltzes around her upstairs room to the latest music, humming the tune as they move. She has to forget it is her late, ex-stepfather, of course, so she imagines real hard that it is Albert returned from the war. She sits at night and stares at herself in the mirror as she brushes her long and beautiful hair; One hundred times she brushes, first one side, then the other. She can hear Albert's voice whispering to her with each stroke of her brush: "You are the most beautiful girl in the world." She blushes a little then, and is careful to keep the hair covering her left ear, at least so she can't see it in the mirror. Then she rises from her vanity table, and climbs into bed, hoping she doesn't have the recurring nightmare about Albert, the one where he is floating down a river under its icy surface. He is dead in the dream, though magnificently preserved, just floating, looking peaceful but lonely. She shivers and climbs beneath the covers. Perhaps she'll get a letter soon, tomorrow maybe. Or soon the war will end and Albert will return. With these thoughts she closes her eyes, and a smile gently forms upon her lips.

The Burial

Something had gone horribly wrong. I heard the dirt being thrown in on top of the pine box. I came to a groggy realization, as the sound became clearer and clearer to me: I'm being buried alive. A moaning, high-pitched squeal escaped my throat, heartfelt terror. Another shovel full of dirt. And then another. Panic washed over me as I tried desperately to stem its tide. I must not lose my head, I thought. Oh, just my life. Just my life. That's what I'm losing. The fear. No, true wretched, insane horror. That's what it is. Can you imagine? Another patter of dirt, and again, and again, it was maddening. What was happening? Plumpf, rattle. What had happened? Still the dirt came falling, crumbling, rumbling onto the top of the coffin. I was sick. The drug had worn off. I wished it had not. I was groggy, unclear of one thing. The all-important question of -- What the hell happened? Another shovel full of dirt fell. Plumpf, rattle. And again. Plumpf, rattle. There were other questions too, of course. Why had I volunteered for it? Why? It had been an insane plan, totally mad. Why couldn't I have seen it then for what it was? I began to think of all the people I would never see again: My mother, my father, my brother, Clem. And Meg. Oh. I would miss her dearly. Would she miss me? Plumpf, rattle. I pictured her sobbing at my funeral. Funeral. There was no funeral, for I was being buried at this moment. Oh God, NO! I began to suffocate. Plumpf, Plumpf, rattle. Plumpf, rattle. The air was close and tight, becoming heavy with a wetness that pressed down on me. My chest began to heave. The darkness. I clawed at the inner lid of the box. No use, I thought. Don't panic. Please. Wait! The rhythm of the dirt being thrown on top of me had broken, ceased. I waited, called out: "Hey! Hey!" And louder still,

The Burial

"Help! Please! In God's name--Please stop!" I waited, listening. No sound came. Then the piling in of dirt came again. It was softer now, more of the box covered. Soon it would be completely covered. My death. Slow death, would come. I banged at the top of the lid again. Yelling, screaming, shrieking. "Murderer! Murderer!" I beat as fast and furiously as I could. Screaming, yelling. It was no use. The dirt still piled up. I could sense its weight on the top of the box, the lid straining beneath it, sagging in on top, bowing, not much, just a little. It was still sturdy, I thought. Too sturdy. I remembered the trap door then. It was the end by my head. How could I have been so stupid? In such a panic. I wanted to laugh. I wanted to cry. Hurry, I thought. I must hurry. I released the latch, but the door didn't swing. It couldn't. It was in a hole. The sides of the hole were against its opening. I was supposed to have sprung the latch and snuck out before it was put in the ground. That was the plan. I was supposed to have done it behind enemy lines, deep behind enemy lines. That was the plan. Not, in the ground. Not deep in a hole. Of course, the box wouldn't open in the ground. The dirt was packed solidly around the thing. The top was sealed tight, like a real coffin. I was supposed to sneak out the end, the end. What had happened? Dear God; What had happened? Surely someone remembered me? Someone was aware that I was trapped. Certainly, they would come, rescue me. Yes! Of course! I listened. Waited. Plumpf, came the soft earth on top of me. Plumpf! Plumpf! A steady rhythm. It continued. But wait. I heard a slight rattle still of small clumps and pebbles rolling on the edges, down the sides. Oh God! Please! Please help! Please! I prayed. Still the Plumpf continued. I lay quiet. It was no use. The plan. The plan had been a dismal failure. I had failed. We had failed. I must pay the price. Plumpf. I held my breath, wondering how long it would take before I suffocated in this thing. Plumpf. I could hold my breath no more. Plumpf. I let out a burst. My chest heaved. It felt as though it were caving in upon itself. Plumpf. Suddenly I was gasping for air, seeking it furiously, frantically, sucking at it. It was wet, moist, non-existent. Already? So soon? Just moments before I had resigned myself to death, given up life for good. Now once again I was clinging

The Burial

to it, grasping for any shred of hope, any succulent morsel of air, as though it were crumbs and I a starving man. I am. If only the drug had been longer lasting? If only the Doc had given me too much of it? I would have been dead already, before being buried. Plumpf. Why me? Why? I had volunteered, yes, unofficially. I was the only one who had known the layout. We were to go well beyond enemy lines. I was dressed in the garb of a Union General. All of us were dressed in Union uniforms. We had practiced it so perfectly, so precisely. What had happened? The drug had worked. I had been out promptly. My body functions had slowed to a standstill, which had helped me to not use up all the oxygen in the box. It worked just as the Doctor had said it would, or so I imagined. How did I know, really? I had not panicked. We had practiced it for weeks. I had lain in the box for hours, days, weeks. The lid would be put on, never completely fastened until the last time. We practiced and practiced, over and over. It should have worked. It was to be easy. There were six of us, five minor officers traveling with the body. We were supposed to make it all the way to the camp, to

Grant himself. It was to be a two-day trip. I was to slip out the second night and sabotage, wreak holy havoc on them. We would all do the same, working together. Together. What had happened? Plumpf. The sound was softer now, muted even more, but still loud enough. Then quieter, and quieter still.

A drop of condensation dripped upon me. The air was close now, very close and tight. I could no longer hear the soft plodding of the dirt upon the top of the coffin. I became sullen, but then a peaceful feeling crept over me. My mind began to play tricks, I heard voices. Dead voices, I imagined, calling me. "Come to us," I heard them say, and their arms were outstretched towards me. Their fingers brushed against me. Certainly, I was dreaming now, the lack of air had done it. So, this was death, I thought. Still not completely sure, still uncomprehending. "Come to us," I heard again, softer and softer the chorus, hypnotic, the fingers, bony, touching me now, clasping, reaching, fondling me, working my flesh, the veil had been lifted. So, this is it? I thought. No more wonder and intrigue. No more trials and tribulations. No more struggle. No more pain. Only the fingers, clawing, grasping, ripping at my flesh.

The Burial

"Come to us," the soft chorus spoke. I looked around at the faces; I could see them now, clearly. I remembered. I had been to Chancellorsville, witnessed the burning flesh. Smelled it. The faces looked familiar here. Why was it so comforting, so soothing? The faces, fingers, voices, "Come to us!" Again, the refrain. The faces were bright, bony, smiling, fleshless. The bony fingers grabbed at me, ripping me, beyond my clothing, beyond my flesh, into my soul. "Come to us!" It became a chant now, more incessant, more rapid, less comforting: "Come to us! Come to us! Come to us! They were turning me over and over now, grasping, grabbing, clawing, spinning me round and round in the coffin, I couldn't breathe, oh, Oh, Oh No! Help! Help! Help Me! I was awake again, still in the coffin, scratching, clawing at the lid like never before. I felt super human. I would have to be. Somehow, I had to escape! Somehow. Some way! I had to! The sounds came again. Dirt. How was it? It was different, the sound. It was getting louder and more scuffled, closer. Again, and again it came. Closer, stronger, louder. The hard scuffle of dirt being scooped off of the top of the coffin. I wanted to scream. I couldn't. There was no air. If I could have screamed, I wouldn't have been able to hear the sweet sounds of dirt being scraped off the top of the coffin. Oh, sweet, sweet, precious sound. The scrape, ever joyous, ever increasing, ever scraping, louder and louder until finally it stopped. It stopped. I would have sucked in my breath had I had any. The hands waited in the darkness. The voices had stopped completely. I listened. The creak and splinter of the lid being prised up, loosened. The hands receded. Prised again, the lid, creaking open, wide this time, completely open, with a joyous swooshing inrush of AIR. Sweet, succulent, beautiful, fantastic, wonderful AIR!

I sprang from the coffin in one jump, as though on springs, or propelled by some superior force, knocking over completely those who had saved me, Choking, Panting, Gasping, Breathing. "Thank You!"

I lay on the ground. Only feet from my death bin, my coffin, Hell itself. Still panting, gasping, relishing every breath. I looked around. Someone lay close to me, unconscious. I recalled a scurrying sound as if someone were running away, screaming!

The Burial

It wasn't me. I was here. It was someone else, screaming madly, running, terrified, flailing through the woods. I looked down at his accomplice. He had fainted from fright. Marauders, Grave robbers, I laughed. They couldn't even wait until the coffin was completely buried. The gravedigger lay close by, he had merely stopped for a smoke and they had clubbed him over the head. Thank God!

Someone was running fast towards me. It wasn't the grave robber returning. It was Marius Early, my close companion, my best friend, my compatriot in the scheme gone awry. He had been charged with watching the casket and busting me out at all costs. If anything happened to foil the scheme, he was to be there. He had promised me he would be. And here he was!

"Thank God!" He hollered. "You're out!" He was bent over, breathing hard from the run. "We were attacked by our own compatriots, a band of Confederates!" He exclaimed. "They saw the Union uniforms and started firing. They had us pinned. They thought they had a bunch of real-life Yankee officers. We couldn't do anything. They shot Vance cold dead, captured Billy and Raif. It was all I could do to escape with my life." He looked me over now, unable to fathom how I appeared, certainly incapable of knowing what I had been through, and definitely unaware of how I felt at this moment. "And Alford?" I asked.

He shrugged and shook his head. "I don't know." There was a pause. An uneasiness began to settle over him. "I circled back and the casket was gone," he continued. "I was out of my mind. I didn't know what had happened to it. But praise the lord you are okay, you got out! I found you!"

I smiled.

He gave a nervous laugh.

I opened my arms. He came immediately into them, much as a brother would. I held him close and then pushed him backwards, tripping him, tricking him, down into the coffin. I pounced upon the lid, pushing it down upon him. I was larger, stronger. I ignored his screams, his ranting, as I hammered away at the lid. Immediately I began shoveling dirt into the hole. Unlike the gravedigger, I didn't stop to have a smoke. I finished the job and sat looking at my fingers, splintered to the

The Burial

bone from scraping the casket lid. I was much stronger now, wiser. I was sure it would have the same effect on him. I looked at the sleeves of the uniform: tattered and torn, and decided to go and clean up. I would get a bite to eat afterwards. That should be about the proper amount of time, not the same as the amount of time I had been buried, of course, but then I didn't want to be overly cruel. And then, perhaps I would return and dig him up, provided, of course, I didn't fall asleep from exhaustion first.

The Owl Tells a Tale

A man's imagination can play more tricks on him than a barrel of monkeys. Especially on the Louisiana bayou late at night. It happens to be a Saturday night in the year 1863. A Confederate soldier is floating in a canoe, moving slowly downstream, working his paddle from side to side. The moon is riding high in the sky, full and shining bright. I'm not quite sure what he is doing here, (not the moon, but rather the Confederate soldier) but I intend to find out -- Or rather, Ahh-hum (I have to clear my throat to find the right voice for the telling of the tale) "I reckon, I aim to find out." Or something like that. There is an adventure afoot in any case (and now I sound like Dr. Watson in a Sherlock Holmes adventure (which has yet to be written) - may this one only work out as nice and tidy). So down I swoop. I come up short on the first try, so I have to circle round again. Usually I'm much more agile, and graceful in flight. I fear I'm getting too old for this . . . Ah. Here we go, a perfect landing, right on the far seat board in his canoe.

"Who!" I say.

He leans forward, then back again, rubbing his eyes. There is the clang and shuffle of him resting his paddle across the canoe. He spits a chaw of tobacco over the side, before speaking.

"Owl, whachoo doin' here? I ain't no pussy cat." His voice is very Louisiana Bayou, don't you think? He swings at me with his oar as he brings it up and over the other side of the canoe. There is a plop sound as he dips it in the water. I have to chuckle to myself at his allusion to the nursery rhyme. I imagine we make quite a sight from afar with the moon as our backdrop. Though his back is rounded, and perhaps I guess, he could be mistaken for a feline from a very great distance. It would have to be a very great distance indeed.

"Who." I say again.

He tries to ignore me then. I calmly watch him, his knobby, arthritis laden knuckles, working the paddle. He is much older than I thought. His back is hunched, and on his head, he's got a large, floppy hat. In fact, he is not the Confederate soldier at all. The Confederate soldier is lying in the bottom of the canoe, wrapped in blankets, or a kind of bag tied with rope. The soldier's legs extend up over the board upon which I now sit. He is starting to squirm now, as though just waking up and realizing he is trapped in a rug (bundled up tight, like a snug bug in a rug.) Well, okay. I'll just stick to my "whos."

The old man seems unconcerned about our soldier's movements. I guess I shouldn't call him 'our' soldier, until we find out a little more about what's going on here. After all, he could meet his demise early on, and not be the main hero of this tale after all. We'll see . . .

And so, our story unfolds . . . Let me fly away to where I'm not a distraction. The narrator of the story should not impinge upon it, or interfere with the reader's concentration. So, I am off with a final: "Who." The old man barely notices as I fly away. Don't worry, I'll still be around, just finding a better seat, some out of the way branch. The old man better be careful he doesn't spit his tobacco into the eye of some crocodile.

He spits, squirting the juice high and over the side. A croc slides into the water, another follows. The swamp is very much alive tonight. The soldier squirms in the canoe, and the old man continues to row. First one side, then the other. Gently. No hurry, it's a beautiful night. Quiet . . .

Two hours earlier, several miles upstream at a stately, Louisiana home:

Another carriage pulled up in front of the mansion and a fine-looking elderly couple got out. They were not the first to arrive at the Howarth's party, nor would they be the last. The party was in full swing, however. The doorman smiled and nodded to the couple, then bowed graciously and waved them in the door. A young man, a soldier, was trying to argue his way into the party. The man guarding the door merely sighed and shook his head at the young man.

"Wait, wait, I can prove it – I've been invited." The young man fished in his pockets, but seemed unable to find what he was searching for.

"I'm terribly sorry, sir, but this is a private gathering." Saying this, the doorman turned and nodded to two ladies of about mid-thirties and ushered them in the door with a very wide smile. They glanced at the young man and then looked at each other with raised eyebrows. Lifting their skirts, they then vanished into the lighted environs. Music drifted out and another, younger lady started to enter with her mother. This younger lady stared openly at the young soldier. He was rather handsome, with sandy, dark blonde hair. He held his cap in his hands and a shock of hair fell freely across his forehead, almost covering one eye. He glanced at the girl from beneath his hair. His glance was momentarily playful, from flashing, dark eyes. The young girl tripped and a slight squeal escaped her lips. It wasn't for the boy, however. It was because her mother had caught her looking at the lad and pinched her arm. However playful his momentary glance was, there was a seriousness surrounding it. He had to remain serious, as he was involved in serious business. He needed to get in to see the colonel, urgently.

"Sir," the doorman said, stepping toward the young man. "I--"

"Wait," the young man said, bending and picking up a small, folded piece of paper from the ground where it had fallen out of his cap. Here it is." He was smiling now, yet still trying to maintain his serious attitude. He unfolded the paper and handed it to the doorman as people streamed past them into the house, greeting several others who were leaving. The doorman didn't seem to notice as he studied the paper.

He looked up from the paper and shrugged. "So?"

"So."

"It's not an invitation, sir."

"But it is on the Colonel's stationary."

"Yes, but--"

"Well?"

"It's not an invitation." The doorman was serious now, handing the paper back to the young man.

A young girl was backing out of the front door giggling as she backed. "I promise, I'll dance with you, later, just let me get some fresh air. It's so stuffy--" She backed right into the doorman, bumping his arm. "Oh, sorry, Vincent, I--" She looked at the young man and stopped. "He's with me," she said.

"But, Miss, I--"

"I invited him."

The doorman looked at her, obviously perplexed.

"We ran out of invitations." In the awkward silence she shrugged.

The young man looked at the doorman, and the doorman looked at the young man, then back at the young lady.

Before either man could respond, the young lady grabbed the young man's arm and led him inside. The doorman shrugged off the odd thoughts that flitted through his mind and went back to greeting the other arriving guests.

Once inside, the girl continued to pull the young man, guiding him through a throng of people. The noise was deafening. There was a tremendous amount of chatter and cigar smoke. The music stopped, there was a clang of instruments, cymbals and brass, and then the music started again. The crowd seemed to be riding high on something, something besides alcohol.

The young man leaned in close to the girl, shouting in her ear. "I need to see the Colonel!"

"Everyone does."

"What?"

"I'll take you to him!"

The boy nodded in understanding. He followed easily along after that. The room was hot, the humidity lingering, a major guest at the party. It almost dripped from the high chandeliers, mixing with the cloying smoke and noise. The cooler air stayed outside, sans invitation. The young man's uniform was sticking to him. He trailed the girl, following close, her perfume mixing with what little air there was. She slid her hand down to his and pulled him onward, perspiring fingers entwining as they moved. She stopped and he ran into her backside.

The Owl Tells a Tale

She turned her head to the left, her hair brushing across his cheek and nose. Her earring grazed his lower lip. An awareness rose up between them, a mild, fleeting feeling. A couple pushed by in front of her. She leaned slightly more into him. He felt the hardness of her earring digging into his lip. He turned his head upward and the softness of her earlobe brushed lightly across his mouth. She shifted. As the couple passed, the woman's hand bumped into the girl's arm and a drink spilled, the glass breaking on the floor. The woman giggled and the man cursed.

"Have you seen the Colonel?" the girl asked the man. He looked at her with bloodshot eyes, a misty, murky look. The eyes were large, shadowy caverns surrounded with crevices of age, cheeks with vessels pushing upward from beneath. The smell of alcohol came off of him in waves.

"No, Missy," he mumbled. Drunkenly, he yanked his wife along. The girl moved forward, after they had passed, pulling the young man on once again.

Eventually they made it across the large room of the swilling, swaying mass of people. The girl opened one of two large doors that met at the center of a doorway. She pushed him inside. "You'll be safe in here," Having said this, she disappeared.

Nerves. That was probably it. It was a collective gathering of people trying to fool themselves and everyone else that they were having the time of their lives. The young man sensed it now. They each had flitted nervously about, drink in hand, speaking gaily, and laughing extra loudly. While in the midst of it, he could feel the tension. It rode across the tops of the alcoholic sea, across the music. The war had been going on for some time now. No longer were people so confident. No longer were they bragging that it would be over in "mere weeks." They knew better now. There was a fear lingering. Nerves were starting to fray. Tempers flared up at small annoyances, like springs popping suddenly from mechanical devices. And all those gathered round were like so many toads jumping from one lily pad to another, each toad's hind leg slipping up to the body after a jump, or just sliding backward off the pad before each lunge, leaving a dewy trail of fear. The languid, dreamy days were numbered now. The parties would soon cease. The young soldier started to open the door and peek back out at the rumbling, broiling sea. He didn't. Instead, he turned and looked about him, surveying the room in which he now stood.

His eyes didn't adjust to the darkness right away. He brought his arm up and wiped his wet shock of hair up across his forehead. He felt the wetness of his fingers as he rubbed them together. Bringing the fingers up to his nose he smelled the girl on them, her perspiration, her perfume. He wiped them on his pants, reluctantly, not really wanting to rid himself of her. Slowly, his eyes began to adjust. There was a gas lamp, turned low. It sat on a desk, a desk he presumed to be the Colonels. A large painting of the Colonel hung just above the desk, flanked on either side by books. Adjacent to the desk, to the young man's left, was a divan. It faced away from him, it's back rising up out of the darkness, higher in the middle and sloping downward ornately on each side. A high-backed chair stood regally at each end. Beyond this was more darkness. He felt the door open behind him, the sound of the party rising up and coming into the room. He turned as it softly shut. The girl stood before him. She let out a breath.

"What a mess out there. Anyway, the Colonel should be here shortly. Want a drink?" She moved over to a side table. In the muted glow he could make out the decanter. Light touched lightly on the girl's cheek and the back of her pale neck. He could sense that she was flushed. The hair stood up on the back of his neck.

"Do you know why I'm here?" he asked.

She didn't respond at first. Then she merely said, "yes." Her voice was soft, not unpleasant. She turned and brought him his drink. She looked at him. Her eyes were large and brown. The muted light hovered in them, much like it rested on the decanter. Her eyes shifted slightly as she viewed his face, another light, only slightly brighter, sliding out from beneath the softness of the lamp's reflection. "Yes," she said again.

"The message said 'Urgent.'"

"Yes."

"On the Colonel's stationary."

She nodded.

"But why did you tell the doorman that 'you' invited me?"

She just looked at him for a second. "I did."

The Owl Tells a Tale

She took a step toward him. "How else would you have gotten in?"

He looked at her. She was close.

"Yes, then, but . . ."

She looked at him, moving closer all the while.

"You invited me? How? I mean, the letter . . ."

"A sham," she said. She kissed him.

He stood still. She kissed him again. Pressing into him, smoothly, firmly.

"A ruse."

"A sham? A ruse?"

"Hm. Yes."

He found himself kissing her in return. He began to lose himself in the moment, lose himself to her. The mechanics of her dress were unique. Though it appeared to be of the usual hoops and corset type structure, it was truly no such thing, more like a woman's fan, with thin wooden slats. It folded around her. With a snap and a twist, it was on the floor. They were in each other's arms again.

"But wait," he found himself saying. "I really do need to speak to the Colonel. There are men, as we stand here now. . ."

He stopped long enough to kiss her. Her fingers were running upwards, through his hair. Then he continued, ". . . plotting, devious, dangerous men."

"If you don't hush, I'll holler out that you're attacking me, or claim that you're a spy!" She kissed him again.

The door burst open, a woman's shrill laugh. Light and music poured into the room. It was the woman from before, and her husband. He stood just behind her. They looked at the young soldier and the girl.

A loud belch broke the stunned silence in the room while the music played in the outer environs riding atop a din of voices. A head appeared above the back of the divan, someone awakening from a drunken stupor. The resemblance was that matching the painting above the desk, and the large brown eyes looked much like his daughter's. The flush cheeks . . .

The Owl Tells a Tale

Back to the owl and the current situation:

Well, ahem! It seems I've found my voice, not to mention a yarn which needs unraveling. You can imagine what happened next, and all the events which led to the current situation. I can skip a few minor details in between. I'm swooping back down now to see what gives. There's a bit of wiggling goin' on in that sack. Whew, just made the edge again. "Who!" That's what I mean to say, not "Whew." The old man's pullin' the paddle out of the water. He's movin' it slow-like, thinkin' I don't see. I won't stay long. He's hefting it high into the air now, menacingly brandishing it. I'm not sure he's gonna really swing round with it – oops! I guessed wrong on that score. Up and away I go. Look at him, he . . . he What? The man dropped with a thud. Just now. Did you hear it? Hm. He's not moving. He's just lying there across the bag with the kid in it. Heart attack maybe. Oh, bejeesus. That boy's really struggling underneath. Well, he stopped for a minute or so, trying to figure what's goin' on. I'm not sure I know even. I'm thinking heart failure. Well, I guess I better do something to help this kid out. I really hate steppin' into the story like this, but there isn't much else to be done at this point. I was the one caused this in the first place. Let me just go down and see if I can find a loose thread or something on the bag. Let me turn my head around and try and see something here. Let me think. Well, yep. There's just a small bit of thread, and yoowho—it's right near the man's machete, right beside him.

THUD.

What's that? Oops. Here I go up, up. . . Oh, I see. The man's arm was hanging off the side and the crock came up and gave it a snatch. He bumped the boat. The kid still doesn't know what's happening. I can see from here though. That darn crock is lunging for it again. The man's arm, I mean. By Jove! This time he got it. He smacked the boat another good one, but he got the arm. Whooh! The kid's lying still now. 'Fraid to move, I guess. I hope that kid gets moving again. Soon. If that crock gets the old man pulled over and drags him off below, that kid will have lost the machete. I'm not sure how much help I can be to him then. There. There you go. That's it boy. Easy does it. We may not be in the big easy, but we're damn close. That's it boy, you got it. I can see your fingers workin' just were I pulled up the thread. Yep. You found it. Great. I see your wrist now. You're close. Yessir! WhoWhoo! You're only inches from the machete now. There you go, you're touching it boy. There, there. You got it. Oh, you dropped it. And here comes that crock again. Bam, right into the boat. Still he can't nab the old buggar. He can't quite get him out of the boat. The moon's shining mighty bright tonight and I can clearly see the old man's nub hanging over the side. He's kinda half up on the seat though, along with lying atop the boy. I hope. Yeah, there you go. You snagged it. Now jiggle that machete loose before that crock jiggles the old fart loose of the boat. Yeah, that's it. You got it. I see you rippin' it yep. There you go. Now use your other hand now you got it free. Oh, here comes that crock again. Another run and he may get the man. His nub's in the water now and he's leaning way over, closer than he was. The machete still isn't completely loose from him yet, but you usin' it. That's it. You got it. Free at last. Yep, Bam. The crock strikes again. Still no success with getting the man overboard. He's tryin' though. And you're out! Yes, you are! You are home free. BAM! And the crock strikes again. And he strikes out again. Well, now that you're up and out, boy, grab that machete. Take hold and just yank it loose of the old man's belt there. Yep! Yep! There you go. You ain't no fool after all. Yo mama didn't raise none! Yep. You got it. She's a loose. Now when the crock comes in again you give that old man a good kick and send him on his way. That crock's got business to attend to with him. I understand you gotta rest some after the struggle getting' out of the bag. But, hey, looky there. Here he comes again. And you ain't even lookin'. Just raise your head boy and give a good lookin' out. Cause he's comin' round again. Yep! Bam. And the man arches up and falls back. Thud. Did that wake you, son? I know you tired, but you can rest later. You got a little time comin' but later it is, not now! There you go, now you stirrin' I know you's tired. I know you's jes as tired and about to plum give out. Just give that man a heave ho there and you home free. There you go, pick up the legs and yep, KERPLUNK. He's in the watta! Yes sir. The old miserable lump a nuthin' has seen better days.

The Owl Tells a Tale

Now his butt is dinner for the crock. He shouldn't a give that spit over in the crock's direction. And he shouldn't a taken a swing at yours truly. . . but, well. That's the way the story unfolded. You saw it.

In any case, boy, the sun's about to put in an appearance. It's just around the next bend, just over them there trees to the east. You just hang tight and row a little when you can. You use that machete if you have too. There, I see that sky startin' to turn. Just a little lighter, not much, but just a little, soon it'll be grayin' up. It'll get just as gray as that old man's unshaved face. Yeah, I can see it. I can feel for ya kid. That young Missy got you in all sorts of hot water with the Colonel. Any business you got to attend to that involves him, why you best send someone else to attend to it. You've had a long night and you's in need of a little rest. Well, you do just that, now. I'll shoo these people away. Or I'll just sit here quiet-like until the dawn comes and then I'll be off. I'll be off until the next tale. Maybe you in it and then maybe you ain't. Who's to say?

Just Plain Bad Luck

"Why, you ain't just gonna shoot 'im, are ya Hawl?"

"Yes, I truly am, Billy!" Hawley waved the gun around in the air as though shooing away flies.

"Well, what about him?" Billy asked, motioning toward the man atop the horse. The man on the horse looked half-dead, bone tired. He was slumped forward, his hands tied to the saddle pommel.

"Why you so worried about that Yankee, Billy? He ain't been nothin' but trouble since we found him. I'm sick and tired of you, him, and this whole dang war. You're startin' to sound more and more like Sgt. Tibbis. Ain't that why we left in the first place? Why we deserted? Ain't you tired of it all? I just want to go on. Not too much longer and we'll be home. I don't even know what I let you talk me into pickin' up this yank for. He's half dead – just look at him!" He waved the gun again.

Billy just snorted and shook his head.

"Well you know I got to shoot him, Billy. He's done broke his leg. Look. He can't even put his foot to the ground. You expect him to stumble around on three legs? How far you figure he'll get, and with a yank on top? You know I gotta do it."

Billy sighed in agreement. "At least just let me get the yank down."

Hawley looked away, up at the sun, and then back down, his head cocked at an angle squinting at Billy. He nodded and then studied his brother. An amused glint formed in his eyes, and his lips twitched into a slight smile.

Billy took out his buck knife and started working at the ropes. The ropes had tightened a bit since he had put them on. He had talked Hawley into letting

Just Plain Bad Luck

him change the ropes to the front just the day before. The man's hands had been tied behind his back initially, but he was so weak, he couldn't balance himself. He fell off twice before they switched them to the front. They probably just should have tied him across the horse's back and been done with it. It didn't much matter now – kaBOOM.

The gunshot sounded, no more than a foot from Billy's ear. He hadn't even seen his brother's arm come up before the gun fired. The horse toppled to its right, over the side of the steep incline, still not fully dead, pulling the rider along with him. They were there one minute, and gone the next. With a scuffle of its legs, the horse caught Billy in the shin with a hoof. Billy was already diving instinctively away when the leg flailed out. He had seen the horse look at him, its eye bulging wide with terror as it went down, slobber flinging from its mouth, blood spurting from the wound. The panicked animal went toppling, struggling, not understanding, but terror-stricken, over the edge.

"Aaw, ... Aagh!" Billy groaned, rolling around in the dirt. "You stupid son of a bitch - - Aaw! Now I think my leg's broke."

His brother came running up to him. "I'm sorry, Billy, really I am!" He was grinning, almost ready to burst into laughter. He wasn't sure how bad he had hurt his younger brother. He guessed he needed to find out. A little hesitantly, he tested: "Billy, here, lemme have a look see. It prob'ly ain't nothing, just a li'l banged up is all." He moved a little closer, still unsure, smirking. His brother was in too much pain to even look up at him. Gradually, he eased closer in and helped Billy up. He helped him to his horse, and hoisted him up onto it. Billy yelped in pain as he flung the bad leg up and over the horse. Just the movement was enough to make him call out.

"I really am sorry, Billy, truly." Hawley looked a little sheepish. When Billy looked at him, he turned abruptly and climbed up on his own horse. They sidled over to the edge and looked down. "I guess we should have saved the saddle and bridle at least. That would have been something." Billy gave his brother an angry look, before wincing in pain. Then he reined in and turned his horse back in the direction they had been heading. Hawley leaned and spit tobacco juice over the edge then turned his horse and began to follow his younger brother. "At least he did have his own horse. It was a fine one too, at least before going lame."

The dying horse twitched convulsively, involuntarily, and slid another ten feet down. Whatever bit of life there was left was escaping. The man's foot was finally freed from beneath it, from the stirrup. Billy had gotten the rope loosened just enough that it slid off of the saddle horn as the horse tumbled. Man, and horse tumbled together, the horse's weight pulling them both down with great speed. The two tumbled one over the other, the horse's weight shifting and turning just enough that even though it landed on the man, it was pulled away again just as quickly as though a gust of wind, or a large hand were blowing or pulling it onward. Grass, rock dirt, man and horse, all moving together as one, then in stops and starts. The man caught, being pulled down, then snagged, his arms above his head, his hands, still tied together, caught, snagged on a branch growing out from the side of the incline.

The ledge hadn't been a straight drop, but steep enough. In places it was sort of level, with loose stones and dirt. As the animal slid, dragging him, the man's foot caught in the stirrup, his hands snagged above, he could have easily been pulled apart. In stops and starts, had he been more aware, he would have felt the snags and branches, brambles and crevices, rocks digging into him, grinding, gouging. All was silent now, however, as the animal lay about twenty feet below the man in what appeared to be a ravine. Below that, there was another, steeper drop. But all motion had ceased. No more falling endlessly, man and horse. Man, nor horse were moving. All was silent. The bright, early afternoon sun cast a harsh light on the scene; a scene now suddenly peaceful, eerily quiet. There would be a silent period, all nature holding its breath, waiting for a sign of some kind, then a sigh, a wisp of breath, and nature would venture forth, tentatively. There would be a call of a bird, then the swish of a squirrel's tail as he stops to listen, watching, an acorn held firmly in his grasp. Another chirp. More movement, a fox moves stealthily along its chosen path, a small rabbit hops twice and disappears down

Just Plain Bad Luck

its hole and a snake slides under the edge of a rock finding a cooler spot. A beetle moves slowly across the mossy area of the rock's underside. The snake touches it gently with its tongue. The beetle freezes. A deer raises its head and sniffs the wind, another bird calls in response to the first and all of nature relaxes, teeming with life.

But the man and the horse are still. The horse lies below, his body cooling in the afternoon sun, a slight breeze helping the cooling process along. The man dangles on the side of the incline above. Time slips steadily by, hours pass, and the light slides slowly away into the darkness. Other creatures emerge, forage, slither about. Life changes. The man still hangs, unmoving; the horse remains still, its body beginning the first stages of decomposition. Ants and beetles crawl into its nostrils and into its open mouth. Several more hours, and the moon becomes full and bright. Restless movement, stretching, awakening, and the night creatures emerge. Exploration and foraging begin. Wolves creep by, heads held low. Coyotes circle about. Raccoons forage. All about the man and horse, nightlife explodes and shifts. The hours continue to pass. Soon the darkness wanes. The moon becomes no more than a paper sheen in the coming light. The purplish hue of daybreak turns to a bright red, then a lighter orange. All is wet with dew. The horse is covered with it, glistening eerily in the morning light. The man is also covered with a thin glaze of it. He hangs totally lifeless, unaware. The morning turns to look upon the day. The sun smiles down. The daylight animals are on the move again. The nocturnal beings are all returned to their lairs. Still the man hangs, and the horse lies quiet. There is movement, as the smaller creatures work on the horse's carcass. The vultures begin to circle overhead.

The man is oblivious, half-dead, lost in the misty dreams and visions of another world. He is lost in the darkness of what awaits us all. He sees things, yet knows not where he is or what these creatures are. He hears children's laughter and is immediately taken back into the land of childhood, running, playing. He hears his mother's voice. She calls to him with open arms. He vaguely knows that he cannot reach her. Mentally he tries. His hand seems to pass through her being. He waits, watching, while

Just Plain Bad Luck

she recedes into the darkness. He hears a flapping, brushing of wings. He sees an angel. A bright light. The angel comes toward him, getting larger as it approaches. It becomes one large shadow with wings. The bright light becomes blocked by the angel; only appearing from behind the winged creature. The light surrounds it. As the angel becomes larger and closer, blocking out more and more of the light, the man has an eerie feeling the creature is an angel of darkness. The light is almost totally blocked out now. He feels a touch on the shoulders, a wing lightly brushing his neck. Suddenly a sharp pain explodes from his cheek as he turns to face the angel of darkness. The bird has just missed ripping the man's eye from its socket. The large black creature starts and flies off, revealing the mid-afternoon sun shining brightly in its wake. Startled, shards of pain racing through his face and body, the man realizes that he is alive, the sun blinding him at first. He cannot feel his arms, yet he moves. He jumps, moving frantically, fighting the pain, ready to fight the bird. But the bird is long gone. Due to his frantic motion, the man's hands have slipped down the branch, the rope holding them together still binding them, but not by much. Billy had cut through some of it, and the branch ripped and unraveled it even more. Still the man hangs, dangling precariously, twenty feet above the dead horse. If he falls, he will probably die. The pain would end, however. He looks up, but can't see anything to grasp. He can no longer feel his hands or arms. He is awake, and alive, but just barely, still delirious. He sees the horse below. One or two vultures had landed and were working on the animal. They seem oblivious to the man's close proximity. It wasn't a vulture that had attacked him. They would have waited. It must have been a blackbird. Perhaps the dew had left a glistening on his cheek that had attracted it. Or perhaps it was the glowing orb of the white of his eye that the thing was going for. He thought it was. It would have plucked it surely had he not turned. Was it instinct that had saved his eye from being plucked and carried away? He looked down, happy to have sight. The horse was moving, twitching with the movement of the animals working at it.

Suddenly the man fell. The rope gave way and he was thrust into the air, descending into the abyss.

Just Plain Bad Luck

He twirled and landed once against the steep incline, feeling the jolt of rock, only mildly softened by dirt which broke loose and fell with him. He felt the agony of a crack, possibly a rib. He hit the incline again and began to slide. When he finally stopped, he lay abutted up next to the horse. He passed out.

He awoke. He didn't know how long he had been out. In pain, he gulped up the air. The stench of the horse was overwhelming, yet he breathed in its sickly-sweet pungent stench with a vengeance. He was alive. Just barely, but alive still. A joyous cackle would have escaped his throat had his lips not been so parched and sore. His throat ached. He could feel the numbness slowly leave his arms and shoulders as the blood seeped back into them. Slowly, he moved his fingers, and then eventually his arm lifted, with tremendous effort, an inch or two. Soon he was able to guide it. A few minutes more, a little more feeling, and he reached. His fingers grasped the inner edges of the horse's belly, the part where the creatures had torn it open. It was wet. He brought his hand back and rubbed the wetness on his lips. He licked his fingers clean and reached for more, this time coming back with a chunk of flesh. It was sustenance, life, and he craved it. The vultures waited patiently, watching from the edge of the clearing. This mad man had interrupted their repast, hesitantly they had moved away, but not for long. They sat in the trees and watched. Perhaps there would be two for dinner. The flies clung to the horse's flesh. The man barely had the strength to brush them away as he pushed the small handful of meat into his mouth. He ignored the maggots further within the gaping hole of the horse's stomach. He felt something jab his side. Looking down at his ripped shirt, he saw a knife. It was caught up in the inside of the material. He had no idea where it had come from. It had cut and scarred his side as he fell, but he hadn't felt it until now. He picked it up and began slicing meat out of the horse's flank. Each movement was excruciatingly painful. He sucked in air, and then worked at the meat. He sucked and chewed heartily on this meal. Not fully satiated, but knowing he could not eat more without resting, he rolled away. He would have to fight the creatures for his next bit of meal, but at the moment he didn't care. He rolled farther away. It was a slow process, but eventually he stopped. The pain overwhelmed him again and he slept.

A few hours later he was awakened by drops of rain falling heavily upon his face. The rain pelted and stung his torn cheek. He turned, looking up into the rain, and opened his mouth wide. This late afternoon shower was a blessing. He pulled himself to where he could lean his back against the incline, and held out his hands cupping them, filling them as best he could. Too much of the water ran through his fingers, escaping to the ground. He looked around, but saw nothing that would help. He tried a small leaf, but it held no more than his cupped hands. He rested, letting the water wash over him. After a while, the rain ceased falling and the sun appeared again, briefly, before descending. The early evening brought a slight chill. He sat, then lay back and fell into a sleep again.

It was early morning before the man woke again. He was a little more rested, but he knew he had to make his way to somewhere else. He had to find a stream, more fresh water, and something to eat. He crawled to his knees, painfully sucking in air between his teeth with each movement and looked down beyond where the horse lay. There was only another drop, this one much steeper. He looked up, no going back that way either. He would have to work around the edge of the mountain somehow, until he found more level footing to search for what he needed. He rose slowly and moved slowly, barely more than a crawl on hands and knees. He had to stop and rest every few feet. With each intake of breath, he felt a searing pain. He looked at his side. Yes, probably a broken rib or two, definitely bruised. Looking back longingly over his shoulder at where the horse lay, he was astonished that he was alive. It was luck that they had landed on the one level ledge that was situated below the fall. He sucked in more air and continued. He leaned back against the least sloping area he could find and reached for foothold after foothold, slowly edging his way. He was ten feet or so from more level ground. It felt as though it might have been five miles. He moved slowly. His foot slipped and rocks tumbled. He took another step and moved as quickly as he could. He slipped again, this time sliding even more. He was now within reach of more stable brush, however. He painfully reached and grasped a small tree and pulled. The pain in his side flashed and stabbed. It jolted him. Angrily, determined, he grabbed another small branch farther up and pulled himself upward. More pain. He almost blacked out again. He could see the horse on the ledge in the distance. He longed for its stability. He would starve there, and die of thirst. He could see the birds working on the horse again. He turned and rested against the tree. If only his strength would hold. He had to move on. He reached, feeling pain, and grabbed hold of another branch, another tree. He edged a foot up and got a grip on the side of the hill, feeling his way upward. He soon found more stable footing, more trees and brush to grasp. After an hour of painful climbing, he was on more level ground, still at an angle, but supportive. He rested, then moved again after twenty minutes or so. Within two more hours he was almost able to stand upright. He could not stand fully erect due to the pain in his side, but he did the best he could. He found a deer trail, and followed it to what he hoped would be water. It was. He was overjoyed. He fell upon the trickle of water and drank his fill. He rested. Waking again, he searched out a bush with berries on it. Seeing where the deer had eaten some of the berries, he felt it should be safe for humans. He ate, and filled his pockets with what he could. He moved on.

Eventually, after another night of sleeping in the woods, and walking, as best he could, stopping periodically to rest, he came to a clearing. There was a small farmhouse. It appeared well kept, but he wasn't sure whether it belonged to friend or foe. He waited, watching. This was Rebel territory, but still there were sympathizers with the Union. Maybe he would get lucky. After all, wasn't he lucky to still be alive? He had been through quite a bit. The fall from the cliff should have killed him, but didn't. The bird should have made off with his eye, but didn't. The vultures should be feasting on his dead carcass right now, but they weren't.

He didn't see anyone leave the small farmhouse. He saw no one arrive either. He rested, watching. He woke in the early dusk. Still he had seen no one come or go. But he had fallen asleep, perhaps then someone had moved and he missed it. He would have to take his chances. The thought of spending another night in the woods without a good meal and in his condition was disheartening. At least he would probably be fed, even if it was by chance the enemy. The prospect was even appealing. He still had the knife, but that was all. He moved quietly toward the house. When he got to the door, he looked about. There was no sound. He pushed on the door and it opened to a warm interior. He shivered and moved inside. No one was around. Then he heard footsteps from outside, coming up on the porch. He had just slipped in and pushed the door to. How could he have missed them?

The old lady was as surprised as he was when she turned. He had grabbed the rifle from her as she turned to latch the door. She had set a bucket of water down before turning. He had snatched the gun away before she had a chance to raise it. She hadn't even known he was there. Once she had made it into the house, she thought she was safe. She looked up at him, appearing weak and fearful. He lowered the gun a little. "I'm not going to hurt you," he said. His voice was weak and not very commanding. He asked if there were any men folk around. She shook her head no. He asked if she was alone. She hesitated at first, then sighed and gave another small shake of her head, this time in the affirmative. He lowered the gun even more.

"You're hurt," she said. She could have been his own kindly aunt, the one who had raised him after his mother had died. "Here, let me help you." She motioned for him to sit down. He obeyed. He leaned the gun against the table, looking up at her. She smiled. She looked at his cheek and touched his wound. She saw him wince when he sat, and seemed to know about his side. "We need to get you fixed up." It wasn't long before she had cleaned and stitched his cheek. She tenderly washed and bandaged his side also. She fed him and let him rest. He tried to stay awake, but after a good meal it was impossible. When he woke the next morning, she had cooked him what little she seemed to have for breakfast. "The one hen we got left didn't lay last night. No egg." Instead, he had a watery stew in a bowl before him. "The soldiers, one side's as bad as the other – all they want to do is rob folks of their food and property as they pass through." She looked at him apologetically, as if suddenly realizing that she was talking to a soldier. She didn't apologize though, not verbally. "That's why I didn't use the lantern last night when I went to put the one cow we still have in the barn. You just can't trust folks – none of 'em." He realized now why he hadn't seen her, and also, why she had probably helped him.

"You want some more?" She asked him, turning to look behind her as the door opened

He instinctively reached for the rifle. She had moved it. He saw it across the room, leaned against the wall. He recognized the faces of the two men standing before him. They had casually walked in bringing supplies from a nearby town. They had probably left the morning before while he was asleep at the edge of the woods, or just before he had arrived at the clearing.

"Now boys," the woman scolded. "You put those guns down."

The two men set the guns aside, just as the old lady had asked. Sheepishly, Billy grinned. His leg was bandaged. Hawley hesitated. "But ma?" he started. Then he just lowered the gun.

"Don't worry," she said. "I've got him taken care of. At first, I wasn't sure whether he was friend or foe, especially when I saw he had Billy's knife on him." She glanced down at the table where the knife lay, displaying the initials B. N. carved into the handle. It was within his reach, but could he get it without getting shot? He looked up at the grinning faces. "He had a yank's uniform on, ripped, torn, and muddy as it was, but who knows these days? The knife had me puzzled. Then I figured 'the only good yank is a dead one!"

The man looked at the bowl. He had eaten all of it except the final spoonful. His head started to spin. His throat became constricted. He began to convulse. Pushing himself up from the table, grabbing for the knife, he spilled the works. The table came toward him, the knife sliding into his lap. He had tried for it and missed. His fingers clawed at the table. He saw the three of them watching him. Their faces were upside down to him as he lay on the floor, gasping for air that wouldn't come. The old lady was watching studiously, still holding the saucepan and ladle. Billy's mouth hung open in shock.

Just Plain Bad Luck

"Now that's just plain bad luck," Hawley said, shaking his head and grinning. "Yes, sir. Just plain bad luck. That's what I'd call it."

The Bugler

Sometimes a dream is just a dream, other times it's something more . . . well, more along the lines of a nightmare. That's still not explaining it though – it's been two weeks. The war is over. That's hard to believe in and of itself. Now I'm back home with my girl. I haven't even told her about this, and probably never will. Hell, no one would believe it. I'm just happy it – he hasn't shown up again. Maybe it's over finally, like the war.

Anyway, I started having these nightmares a couple of months ago. My unit was training, preparing to leave. No, I'm not gonna tell you what unit, nor where we were training. Nor am I gonna just state my name, rank and serial number. Hm. That was kinda funny, right? I oughta be a comedian. Well, anyway, I would be happy to never see this guy's mug again, this bugler.

So, we would be having drills during the day and I was getting no sleep at night on account of this guy. It was never any exact time. It wasn't at the stroke of midnight like in the movies, nor was it at two in the morning. It could be ten minutes to 1:00 or 3:22, or whatever. I guess it was more determined by the state of sleep I was in, what level I was at, see?

Anyhow, I would all of a sudden be brought straight up out of sleep by a bugle sounding reveille, right in my ear, or at the head of my bunk anyway. Loud and clear. This wasn't particularly funny, because reveille would come around soon enough as it was. I would get real angry. I would glare at this guy, but I couldn't ever see his face—but I'll tell you about that in a minute. Just when I would jump up and be ready to wallop this joe he would march straight out of the barracks. I would race after him,

The Bugler

angry as heck, but somehow, he would always be just out of reach. Not way ahead, mind you, but I could never touch him. Same as I could never see his face, only the edge of his chin and part of his left jaw where the moonlight would shine in the window near my bed. The light would touch him just right across it, the bottom edge of his jaw. It was just the spot I would want to give him a knuckle sandwich every time he woke me up with that damn bugle. Well, I say "woke me up," but with what transpired later, I can't exactly explain whether I was asleep or not. But surely, I was, because it wouldn't have got me so sore when he let on with the horn if I wasn't.

Well, whatever you want to call it, I would be chasing him out the door and into the woods and he would just disappear, vanish, just like a . . . well, ghost. I might as well go ahead and spit it out, level with ya. I don't believe in such things, and I would even call you crazy if you told me this tale. Tale, story, dream, whatever – I would still call you loony, and maybe I should be locked away . . .

So, where was I? Oh, yeah, well I would be standing all alone scratching the back of my head and wondering where this creep had disappeared to. I would be wide awake, so to speak, just standing in the middle of nowhere. I would be just out amongst the trees, not too far from the barracks, but far enough. You would think I would be questioning some things, and I was, just the main ones though, the more obvious. I should have been asking things like, well, where was the night watch during all this? Or, what did the rest of the guys see? Were they all sound asleep? And maybe, just maybe I should have taken a good look around at the sleeping beauties and paid a little more attention to what types of uniforms they had on, or whatever. Not that they would have been sleeping in their uniforms or anything, but that's what really creeps me. I just didn't look. But I was tired, see? Real tired. This went on for almost every night. There would be a night or two that he would miss, and I don't know why – maybe he had other business to attend to. I don't really care, those nights were real swell. Those would be the nights I got some sleep. This went on for a month or so. Oh yeah, I was miserable for lack of sleep. And that's another thing, another big question – why me? Of all the guys in this man's army. This man's

The Bugler

as in Uncle Sam's and yours truly, not the bugler's, though I guess he must have been in it too at one point. He just never got out, still serving, forever! Now that's dedication.

So, this was an ongoing thing, pretty much night after night without letup. He would sound reveille and I would be up and after him. He never hurried though. I would be hauling it after him, but he never hurried. He was at a steady march, and I followed, every night. I would never catch him though. He would always be right in front of me, but I would never catch him. He had all the time in the world to march, an eternity (that's a pun in case you missed it. The comedian just comes out in me, but I guess I shouldn't joke about it. It was no laughing matter losing all that sleep).

So, let me get to the punch line – and this is where it really starts to get weird – not that it wasn't pretty weird already, see, but this is the beginning of what it's all about. Here it is . . .

I was out this one afternoon. We all were, just coming back from drill, hot, tired, the works. Percell and I were lagging behind. I lit a cigarette (not that you did that sort of thing in formation, but like I said, we had dropped back. The sarge wasn't looking back anyway). I just started to hand Percy one and he starts in with yappin' about having to use the latrine. This guy's got some kind of bowels, I tell you. "But the barracks is almost in sight. You can hold it, right?" Well, he's off and running, only not towards the barracks. Well, I decide to wait, who knows why? Probably 'cause I was trying to get in good with his sister, but anyways . . . I plopped down on the ground and rested against this rock. Who knew how long Percy was gonna be. I should've left him. I did, in fact, start to get up when I saw a lizard run under the rock. I wanted to see where he went, so I gave the rock a shove. It wasn't a large piece of work or anything, just a rock, maybe a foot across. Well, it didn't move at first, and by now I was standing so I gave it a good kick and then flipped it. More out of boredom than anything was I going after this lizard, not for any special reason. The thing was gone, but I took another drag on my cigarette and looked around for Percy. He wasn't around yet, so I gave a whistle for him to hurry it up. This was when I saw the packet. It was some

The Bugler

kind of oilskin or cloth of some kind, and how what was in it got preserved I couldn't tell you. Well, there were a couple pieces of gold, just a couple of coins, old (and I know how they lasted so don't get funny). It was the other thing, the letter. I don't get that. It had a date on it of 1863, and I could make out some of the writing, not much of it but some. I didn't get much of a chance to check it out because Percy got back about then. The guy had some kind of timing, I tell you. He was pretty curious, but I just told him about the lizard and that was it. I'm not sure why. I guess I just wanted to give it all some thought and check out the coins a little closer. It wasn't until later that I realized the place I found the letter was where I always stopped the chase in the dream. It was where the bugler always vanished. It was where I would always be spent and have to bend over to catch my breath, stitch in my side and all. I would always be right at that rock.

Well, it wasn't until later that I got the chance to check out the items a little closer. The letter was made out to some gal named Celia from some guy named Albert or something. From what I could tell, he thought it was gonna be the last one he would be able to write. He seemed real lovesick though. I kinda felt sorry for him. I mean, that he wasn't gonna be able to see her again. Well, who knows? Maybe he did get back to her in the end. Why did he leave the coins and the letter under a rock though? That was just one more unanswered question. And now I'm coming up on the real goofy part of it all.

That night I put the letter and the coins under my pillow before going to sleep. I could have locked them in my footlocker I guess, but I didn't. I just stuck them under my pillow, like the tooth fairy was gonna come or something. Not that the tooth fairy was gonna take coins. The thing was, I just felt like doing it. I just made the choice, then I went to sleep not thinking much more about it.

The bugler came that night, just like he had the others. Somehow, I just felt him standing there, though, and woke up. I didn't wake up angry. I didn't go chasing him. I just felt him, opened my eyes and looked up. There he was. He started to bring the bugle up to his mouth and then stopped. He looked at me. At least I think he did. He turned his head and the angle of moonlight caught the side

The Bugler

of his face. It caught more of his face than it ever had. It revealed more of it than I ever wanted to see, or ever want to see again. Where his eye should have been was a hole. I wish I could tell you that it was sown shut or something, but it wasn't. I mean, my mind wants to picture it as having been sown up. I can see the stitches in my mind's eye as though it was sown, but it wasn't. There was just a jagged hole. And running up from the corner of what should have been his mouth was a large cut, much like a scar, only it wasn't exactly that. It was more open, like a smile running up the side of his face. How he blew the bugle without all the air escaping out the side of his face was something I couldn't figure out. There was a lot I haven't been able to figure out. I thought I saw the edge of a tooth, maybe a whole row of them, so in my mind he was smiling. Then again, in my mind that jagged hole of an eye was sewn shut too, with the thread squinching it tight and pulling his cheek upward. Was it a smile? Why didn't he play reveille that night? Why did he turn and look at me? Why did the light have to land where it did and show me more of his face? The light showed me another thing I hadn't noticed before. I don't know why I hadn't noticed the Civil War getup he was wearing before then. Maybe it was my anger that got in the way. Maybe it was that and the fact that it all seemed to happen so fast, all the running, the running and not catching him. I just knew that it wasn't anger that night – it was fear! I just lay there as he marched out, too petrified to give chase.

There are still a lot of unanswered questions. The biggest question is what happened to the items I had under my pillow that night? They were gone the next morning. I would question whether it all was just some nightmare I was having just about every night, but I know it wasn't. Oh, I would be asleep and he would play reveille like nobody's business. But it was real, at least some of it, at times. I just haven't sorted it all out yet. If a maniac like Hitler can wreak havoc on the whole world until about three weeks ago, going for four straight years, I guess I can be allowed to have a nightmare be real. All I know is the dreams have stopped, the war is over and I've got some livin' to do. Let the bugler go on about his business. In some far corner of my

The Bugler

mind I'm hearin' Taps sounding on his bugle, but that's just probably my imagination; Same as I'm imagining him climbing back into his grave, the letters in one hand and the bugle tucked up under his arm. May he rest in peace is all I've got left to say.

House of Unspeakable Things

"I'll have to ask the Missus."

"Sure." I watched her walk away. She was an attractive black woman, maybe twenty-five years old or so, hard to tell. I looked back at Billy. He was just climbing down from his mount, holding the reins of mine. My horse snorted and pawed at the ground, a little restless. Looking back inside, I observed the young black woman bending down and conferring with an old woman in a rocker, the Missus. The old woman's back was towards where I stood at the door, both of them were facing away. The rocker was facing the hearth, the black woman leaning over it, the two heads not an inch apart. It was in a back room, with the door standing ajar, and the descending sun's rays didn't extend far enough into the house for me to make out much of anything, but I could just make this out from my angle. The black woman nodded slightly, rose and came back to the door.

"She says it's okay, but jus' one night 'cause we don't want no trouble with the Federals."

"Sure," I said. "Yep, I understand." I was happy about it, couldn't keep from grinning. It had been a long day of riding. I looked toward Billy, and he let out a howl, slapping the reins on the hind quarters of his horse. Dust rose up into the sun shining behind him. The horse reared, and Billy immediately set to calming him, laughing. The horse moved around and bumped into mine, all three turning into a circle, getting tangled, Billy and the two horses. I shook my head and felt embarrassed for some reason. "It's been a long day of ridin'." I said. The woman just gave a slight smile.

"We'll just put the horses up and be right in." I said, giving her a questioning glance.

"Sure," she said. "You's prob'ly hungry." With that she shut the door.

"The old lady must be ill," I said, as we moved off toward the barn.

Billy nodded, the shadows of the tree tops dancing lightly across his face and then sliding across the upper part of the barn. The horse's hooves clopped with soft thuds in the dirt and swirled up small clouds of dust as we went, while their heads were hanging low and nodding rhythmically up and down. I couldn't actually see the dust in the growing darkness, as the sun didn't extend much through the lower part of the trees at the edge of the clearing, but I could imagine it, taste it. I licked my lips and spit. One of the horse's hoofs clacked against a small rock, upturning it a little. The horse snorted. We were almost in total darkness by the time we got to the barn.

I handed my horse's reins to Billy again and lifted the wooden bar from the supports. The barn gave an arthritic groan and a yowl when I pulled the large doors open. From the looks of the thing I would have guessed it was hollerin' for paint. Either that or asking to be torn down. It wasn't in much shape to speak of.

Upon entering its cavernous yaw, we ran into a whole mess of cobwebs, almost thick as carpet hangin' in the air. The webs not so much brushed the cheek as caressed and covered the whole head, encompassing it totally. We clawed at the air until we ripped enough of an opening to breathe. "Gaw'd!" Billy lashed at the stickiness. The horses squirmed and whinnied. "Maybe we should just keep ridin'," Billy mumbled. I could sense something, a tinge of fear, just a touch. There was something akin to it resting at the corners of his eyes when he looked over. I could barely make him out in the darkness, but the whites of his eyes sort of shined with an edge of it. I could sense his nervousness, but there seemed to be no real reason for it. All the same, a tickle rose up, climbing the back of my neck. I tried to shake it.

"No. 'Sides, we got grub comin' if we can make it back to the house."

Billy grinned at that, a little more calm. Once again, I couldn't see it so much as feel it. He had a grin that sort of emanated and floated around him. I could just make it out, lingering in the air. It flashed nervously a time or two and then disappeared.

I felt along the wall and found a lantern. It was sticky and thickly covered with cobwebs like everything else. I lit it and looked around. More cobwebs, not much else. A lonely, haggard bridle hung on a far wall. It too, was covered in web, looking like a cocoon of some kind. "Not much here."

"I'm guessing even the mice have vacated this place," Billy smirked.

"Yep." I went over and looked in a stall. The straw on the ground was sparse. Maybe enough for tonight. "And I believe I saw a well outside."

Billy headed out to get water as I looked around. The barn hadn't been used in a long, long time. Not only had the mice vacated, but there wasn't a single bird or bat in the upper rafters. Billy was back soon enough and startled me when he spoke behind me.

"I'm tired enough," he said. "But I don't know about beddin' down in here?"

"Yeah, well the night looks like it might stay clear. We got our rolls; we can bed out in the open. I don't feel much like sleepin' in here either."

When we got back to the house, the black woman was makin' us something to shovel in. It wasn't much, but sure smelled good. I figured we wouldn't have no trouble at all satisfying our hunger. Some kinda stew, a little short on the beef, but we'd make do. There was some biscuits on the side, in all a hearty meal sure enough. As far as I could tell, the Missus hadn't moved from the rocker. The door was pulled a little closer than before. "The Missus ill?" I asked, nodding toward the door. The woman turned and looked at me for a minute or so before respondin'.

"Oh, she's as good as she can be, and right as rain when she wants to be."

I'm not sure what kind of an answer that was, but I let it alone.

Billy handed me a small bottle of whiskey and I took a swig, tryin' to keep it off to the side and somewhat out of view. It was like the woman had eyes in the back of her head though.

"This is a God-fearin' house gentlemen, but as you're prob'ly gonna do as you please with little or no repentin' there's a bottle round here somewhere that was left when the Master passed on a couple years back." She searched around some, but not too much before she found it. She set a dusty bottle on the table and gave us leave to have at it. She fiddled a bit with a rag she held and then turned again and spoke. "Now, I'm gonna go in and tend to the Missus. When you finish up you can go on upstairs to spend the night. There's two rooms up 'n above, one's used for storage, the other's not bein' used at all. The Missus can't go up anymore and I bed down here to see she don't need nuthin'. Be a sight more comfortable here than in the barn."

"Thank ya, ma'am," I said. "We couldn't ask for much more in the way of hospitality."

"Yes'm, thank ya," Billy chimed.

When she was good and gone Billy and I just looked at each other, both happy at the piece of luck we was havin'. "We couldn't ask for a better setup than this, no siree," Billy beamed, as stew ran down his three-day whiskered chin. He wiped it with his sleeve, and then spoke again, leaning in close this time. "Say, she seems to run the place for the most part, at least with the Missus' say. And she ain't a bad looker neither."

I nodded in agreement, poured us both another shot and grabbed another biscuit off the plate. "No, we coulda' had a much worse night than this. Guess we got lucky. "

"Yep."

We spent the next five minutes or so in silence, broken only with grunts and groans of pleasure. After a few more minutes of drinkin' we sat back and looked at each other. Billy's eyelids were droopin' and I guess mine were about the same.

"Well, I reckon we should go up and check out the room." I ventured.

Billy nodded and we pushed away from the table and made our way up the stairs. We both were tired and the booze was makin' its way through our weariness like a lazily moving stream on a warm afternoon. Time we got upstairs to the room it was all I could do to nudge the door open. There was two small beds situated in a stuffy room. It was small but seemed cozy enough to suit us. We looked approvingly at each other. Billy shunted up the window with no little amount of effort, the wood groaning as he pushed. Once he got it moving though it went up easy enough. We each sat on our respective beds and took off our boots. The window slammed down and gave us a good start when it hit. We looked at each other and waited a couple of minutes. We heard no hue and cry from below, so Billy opened it again. This time he wedged his boot in the space to keep it open. We had a pleasant breeze flowin' into the room after a minute or two. We lay back in silence, Billy scratching his chest and picking at his teeth with a bit of straw. "You know," he said after a bit, "the Missus is real nice for puttin' us up for the night."

I blew out the lamp and lay back. I didn't answer with much energy. All I could manage was a small grunt. I knew more was comin'.

"That other one sure is a looker, ain't she?"

This perked me up some, and I couldn't resist a poke. "Well, Billy, go down and get you a little a that sugar then."

He gave a small snort.

"Just don't let the Missus catch you at it."

Billy laughed. "I expect you'll be keepin' the Missus busy so as she won't notice a thing."

"Sure, Billy. Sure, you just go right on dreamin'."

It wasn't too long before I heard him snoring. I rolled over on my side and closed my eyes.

I don't know exactly what woke me. Could have been a sound downstairs, or maybe it was just nature nudging me. I picked up my boots and snuck on down.

All seemed quiet when I hit the bottom, so I eased on outside. I sat on the porch and put on my boots. The moon was up high and bright, pretty much full. I could see well enough to strike out around the back, wandering off toward the outhouse. After thinkin' on the barn some, I decided to go off into the edge of the wood to take care of business. It was a quiet night, too quiet. Once again, I was struck with the thought that there wasn't much in the way of signs of life on the place, not even crickets chirping, no fireflies, nothing. No frog croaked, nor owl hooted.

I took a notion to check on the horses before heading back to the house. They seemed fine. I reckoned we must be enough out of the way that we didn't have to worry about the federals this night, not unless a stray scout came snoopin' along by chance. Relaxing a bit, I took a smoke before goin' on back inside. The slight breeze was mildly cool, but sticky all the same, and all was dead silent. The silence itself seemed sticky and threatening, like a large, malevolent hand was enclosing about the place with a sweaty palm, the fingers just open enough to let a slight waft of a breeze through. Sweat slid down my spine and I felt a chill. I stepped quickly inside. Taking a look back over my shoulder I had a weird sensation. It seemed that just out at the edge of the clearing there was movement. Still no life, just a slight twitching of a nervous finger, a tick. Something was waiting, waiting patiently for the right moment, the perfect second to catch its prey. I quietly closed the door behind me and came to a decision. I had suddenly decided that Billy and I might need to think about heading out, right then and there. Perhaps I should notify the Missus and thank her for all the hospitality before we left. Then I started to feel a little more comfortable, the unease slowly detaching itself from me and drifting away.

The coziness of the house crept over me, crawling slowly and easily, too easily. I noticed the dishes put up from the table. There was light coming from under the door to the back room.

I approached it, hesitated. Something seemed to be whispering in my ear. Stay. The coziness again, the warmth and hospitality. It was soothing, enticing. I glanced and saw the firelight shining from beneath the door, shifting. Stay, see how cozy, feel the comfort. Maybe I had imagined everything. What had happened? What exactly? Nothing really. I couldn't think of one, solitary bad thing. The cobwebs in the barn. That was all. Absolutely nothing else had happened. Coziness nibbled at my ear, licked at my brain. Stay. Feel the warmth. It's sooo cozy, sooo soothing. The firelight flickered beneath the door. I knocked, not sure what I would say.

"Come in." The voice was soft, melodic. The light flickered. I stood frozen. There was silence. I waited. There was waiting on the other side of the door. Everyone waited, patiently, biding time, waiting on the proper moment.

"Yes?" softer still. Stay. Feel the warmth . . .

I slowly pushed the door open. In the flickering light I could see the woman. She was pulling a blanket around her naked body, holding it with one hand. I moved into the room. She looked at me, no fear, no worry, just a soft, steady glow in her eyes. She was calm, at peace.

"Sorry to wake you, ma'am. . ." I glanced nervously at the old woman in the chair. I could only see the back of her head, a shawl was pulled up and over her cheek, draping the side of her face, covering it. I wondered what sort of illness she had. Perhaps I should just retreat quietly, go back to the room and lie down.

The younger woman leaned down and picked up the poker with one hand, still clutching the blanket with her other one. It slipped a little off of her shoulder as she stoked the embers. The shoulder was bare, shining smoothly in the firelight.

She looked at me, a soft, questioning glance with innocent brown eyes. Stay. I took another step forward, still not sure what to say. My leg bumped the arm of the rocker. Her glance lit nervously on the woman in the chair. I saw fear reflected in her eyes, dancing on the flames and mirrored in them. I tensed, hoping I hadn't woken the old lady. She started to move. The shawl slid off her cheek and I realized she hadn't moved; I hadn't woken her. She would never move, or waken. She was dead. How long had she been dead? Looked like quite some time.

I was stunned, unable to pull my eyes from the old lady, what was left. Her features were a grayish green, with sunken cheeks. What flesh the Missus still had was more drapery than flesh, it hung in folds. Her long, sinewy arms rested on the rocker, rigid, ending in bony fingers gripping the curve of the rocker arm. A ring seemed trapped between bone and wood, encircling one of the fingers. I slowly pulled my gaze away and moved it along the floor. My eyes seemed heavy. With great effort I lifted them, not wanting to meet the younger woman's gaze any more than I had wanted to meet the old woman's. I looked anyway. First her bare feet, then her legs, the edge of the blanket, on up to where she clutched it loosely at her chest. She was raised up a little higher now, the edge of the blanket resting lower on her breast, exposing part of it, still revealing her smooth shoulder, her graceful neck, her cheek and finally her soft brown eyes. Her gaze was still on the woman in the rocker. Stunned, almost as though she had just now realized the old woman was dead, just a corpse. Stay. I glanced back at the rotting, half-mummified corpse. Don't leave. How had I not smelled it? Had I become that used to the bodies on the fields of battle that somehow my sense of smell closed itself off to the putrid scent of death? My sense of smell should have been triggered upon entering the house, right away I should have known. Still, I hadn't sensed it. Stay. I noticed something else at this point. The corpse's mouth was open, as though forming a scream. No sound was coming out. Stay. Don't ever leave. The glint of the firelight played across the opening, revealing something within. A tiny, sack-like silky cocoon hung, dangling at the back of the throat, like tonsils. A spider crawled across the bulbous sack, moving slowly. The sack was torn in a spot and a dark golden substance leaked out. Smaller spiders emerged and crawled around the sack, moving off into the back of the gray throat. No screams. What may have started as one was now frozen in time. Stay. I felt a scream beginning to develop in the back of my throat, yet it wouldn't form, an itch, the sense also of a twitching finger, just a slight tick, waiting outside, just at the edge of the wood.

My breath came in short spurts, not very much air at any one time. I felt I was suffocating. Suddenly I knew what I would find if I ran up to wake Billy. He would be lying there, wrapped up in a silky whitish-gray cocoon, a silk shroud. His breathing would be slow and intermittent, indicated only by the movement of silk covering his mouth and face. The O shaped covering would be pulsating rhythmically in and out, ever so slowly. And the horses would be the same; I could see them lying on the ground, two carcasses with outstretched legs bound in sticky web-like coverings. It would have started in each of the animal's nostrils, a moistness. A gradual thickening of mesh, spreading and thickening until they suffocated and dropped. They would scream and writhe in desperate pleas for air. Gradually, bound by the tensile, sticky webbing, the last breath cut off, all movement would cease. I thought of the barn, the harness, all covered. In my mind, the lamp was covered like a cocoon, yet lit and glowing within, spreading a muted light. Pulsing. I looked again at the tonsil-like sack dangling in the corpse's throat. It seemed a sort of microcosm of the outer world, a crystal ball. I could see myself, the young black woman, the farm, pulsing within the membrane, inside the outer milky thick substance. It wasn't a hand encircling the place at all, but a web being spun, in ever thickening strands, slowly beginning to cut off the air. I pulled my eyes from the old corpse and looked at the woman standing by the hearth. A small wet bead formed on her lower lip and then dripped off of it, dangling spittle-like in the firelight. It swung a little, swaying in the light and then I noticed the small spider on the end, swinging. It wasn't spittle after all. The flames darted and danced in the woman's dark eyes. She gave a slight coughing gasp and another stringy drop swung from her lip. My own lips felt parched. I licked them and took a breath. There was a raspy itch tickling the back of my throat. I felt a need to cough. I swallowed again, trying to fight the urge. My revolver, I thought. I'll have to shoot the woman first. Then I remembered, absently feeling for it, that I had left it upstairs. I coughed and felt a stickiness cross my lips, tiny beads of spittle dangling. I squished as many of the beads as I could between my thumb and fingers. Then another cough came and more tiny creatures flooded up into my mouth, riding a sea of bitter tasting fluid.

I looked at the woman, an intricate mesh forming across her face, thickening. She clawed at it trying to rip holes, but couldn't. She held her throat with one hand while ripping and clawing at the webbing with the other one. Her head rocked from side to side, as she tried to shake it off of her. The meshed webbing was sucked inward with each breath she tried to take, and each outward exhalation of the air that remained within her lungs caused it to puff out. Each spewing of fluid brought a new batch of spiders. They had no problem exiting the membrane covering as they worked diligently at suffocating her. I coughed again, and spewed forth a small army of new laborers. The woman fell to the ground, writhing, the poker lying beside her. I had a sudden flash of insight and grabbed it up. I stood and drove it straight at the globule hanging in the corpse's mouth, the rocker overturned and I toppled onto the corpse. The glowing sack detached itself and rolled onto the floor. It moved and I smashed it. I rose up and stomped it, smearing the contents. Then there was nothing. I coughed and spewed up more creatures. These weren't alive. The writhing continued on the floor behind me. I dove on the woman and ripped a hole in the area that covered her mouth. She sucked in air, coughing and gasping, then slowly clawed away the mask of silk. We both lay on the floor in silence. There seemed to be no more activity of the web-makers. The hours passed, just a couple and the soft light of dawn seemed to slowly rise. I stood and went upstairs. Billy was no more than a husk of a corpse. The window stood open and a small bird alighted on the sill. I went back downstairs and the woman had dressed and was waiting on the porch. She wore a white cotton dress with strawberry designs sewn into it. I guessed it had been the Missus' dress when she had been much younger and definitely much more alive. She wore a bonnet with a wide blue ribbon holding it on. The sun was bright. Birds chirped. Frogs croaked. A rooster crowed in the distance. Neither one of us spoke. We simply walked away from the place in silence. We moved slowly, as though in a stupor, neither fully awake; Neither speaking, not wanting to acknowledge the events of the night. After a time, we came to a crossing in the road. She hesitated. I stopped. We looked at each other and then parted, each moving in separate directions. "God fearing house," I mumbled. She stopped and looked back over her shoulder. A soft breeze moved the end of one of the blue ribbons across her lips and cheek. The edges of her mouth twitched upward, nervously. It was almost as though she wanted to smile, but couldn't. She didn't say anything, but I could hear her thoughts just as if she had. "Guess not," they seemed to softly say. Then we both started moving again. Each one of us was edging toward freedom, neither of us sure we were there yet. Had we reached the outer edges of the web yet? Had the nightmare ended? Was the thing dead? How had it held the woman? How long? Maybe she was moving with a lighter step than I was, more relieved to be free, after being held prisoner for so long. I quickened my pace, nervously feeling for a sticky, web-like substance before me. I raised an arm up in front of me, feeling the empty air, no web-like tendrils met my fingers. I looked back behind me. The woman was long gone. I began to move more briskly, wanting to run, but daring not.

A Blind Eye, a Missing Appendage, and a Friendly Card Game!

"Case dismissed!" The judge slammed the gavel down. The courtroom was abuzz with consternation on one side and jubilation on the other. Surveying the scene with a stern eye, the judge banged the gavel once again. "Order. I say -- order in this courtroom, or I'll hold you all in contempt and throw the lot of you in jail."

The crowd, quiet now, stood staring at the judge, as if frozen in place. They searched his face for any leeway and found none. His bushy eyebrows met in the middle and pulled downward on the ends just above the outer corners of his eyes. His eyes were large, soft brown, usually full of kindness and wisdom. Now, however, they were steely, with a decidedly hard challenge in them. It was a glare he had practiced and perfected over many years of dealing with the most hardened of criminals. He dared anyone to move or speak.

"Now," he said. "You will all file out in an orderly fashion. Quietly. And we will have no more nonsense. None!" He didn't have to raise his baritone voice as it carried naturally, touching on every corner of the room without effort. He had maintained this court for the past seventeen years and would not cater to any foolishness. The townspeople knew him as well as he knew them.

The 'nonsense' the judge referred to was related to the week-long case just ended of **Elk Grove v. DuBarry.** Rather, it was a case against the DuBarry slaves, technically. It was a matter that started out as a simple case of concern for the safety of an

A Blind Eye, a Missing Appendage, and a Friendly Card Game

elderly lady that evolved into a question of what had happened to a soldier's leg. The whole town was in an uproar as absurdity piled on top of absurdity. If it had lasted more than a week there would have been incidents of murder. The mayhem was inevitable. The town's population totaled 600, not including the slaves and indentured persons whom were never counted at all.

The Monday prior, exactly one week ago to the day, the elderly lady in question, Ms. Martha DuBarry took a spill. She was riding into town on the front seat of a wagon, sitting right between her two negro house servants, Morris and Esther. The horses pulling the wagon had stumbled momentarily, and then suddenly lurched forward. Ms. Martha DuBarry spilled over backwards into the back of the wagon and the result was a broken wrist, and a bruised thigh. She could have bumped her head, of course, which seemed to be everyone's concern, and had she been any less inebriated she would have probably sustained worse injuries, possibly even died in the process. As it was, she went heels-overhead and took a backwards somersault into the bed of the wagon. Why Morris or Esther didn't have a hold on her is anybody's guess. Someone said they saw Morris, who was driving the wagon, point toward something in a display window across the street when the horses then stumbled, Esther reached across to gain control of the reins, releasing her hold on Ms. DuBarry. In any case, there was a Deputy walking by and he took an interest in the incident – not only the incident itself, but the whole of the situation with Ms. DuBarry and her two negro companions. Charges of neglect were filed and questions of competence arose. One thing led to another, and the lives of Ms. DuBarry and Morris and Esther Garvin came under intense scrutiny, just as one might observe three insects under glass.

Ms DuBarry retained legal counsel and the case ended in a court battle between the small city of Elk Grove, VA and Ms. DuBarry.

The judge now conferred with the bailiff, and motioned for the counsel for both sides to step forward. When he looked beyond them and saw the townspeople at a stand-still he was a little surprised. "You may proceed," he said. "Remember, in an orderly

A Blind Eye, a Missing Appendage, and a Friendly Card Game

fashion." Everyone seemed to be waiting on the first one to make a move. No one did.

"Go on," the judge said. "Git!" And with that, they all made a move at once for the doors of the courtroom. The judge looked past the two lawyers standing before him and spoke to the deputy sitting in the room. "That includes you, Deputy Cosgrove."

Cosgrove had been the deputy who had witnessed the incident and started the ball rolling. He sat stunned at the outcome of the proceedings. He was a small, wiry, balding man, with puffy, flushed cheeks. Slowly he rose, trembling in a fit of what appeared to be anger and embarrassment. He wanted to speak, but dared not. Agitated, dejected, he made his way to the door, moving at the tail end of the crowd.

"Now Gentlemen," said the judge, smiling. "We can repair to my chambers for a drink and a cigar, to celebrate the end of a very eventful and harrowing week." He might have been inclined to have added the word circus on the end of his sentence, or just between 'harrowing' and 'week,' because that was exactly what it had been over the past week, a mad circus.

Events had transpired over the week that had had all of the town up in arms. The war raging between North and South took on the aspect of being secondary in importance. Everyone in town took up a side. It became known by all, as it had been known by several and heard by many more, that Ms. Dubarry was wont to drink to excess. Her inebriation was not intentional, of course, not at the outset, but it happened all the same. She would start with a drink in the morning and it wasn't long before she was sloshed. One drink having led to two, and then a third, and so on . . . Amazingly enough, she had abstained from any sort of alcohol throughout the whole of the trial. She appeared the model of sobriety the entire week.

The judge looked out into the courtroom. The crowd had finally made its way outside. He then lowered his voice and asked, almost sheepishly, if Ms. Dubarry might be interested in joining the rest of the small party in his chambers. She looked at her two negro companions, who dared not even exchange glances at the moment, cleared her throat,

A Blind Eye, a Missing Appendage, and a Friendly Card Game

and answered the judge with a polite, "well, a small drink to celebrate the outcome of the trial couldn't hurt." The two negroes then couldn't resist a glance at each other when the elderly lady cleared her throat and said decidedly, "I'd be delighted." She rose up and moved toward the circle of waiting men as though she were forty years younger, going to meet a group of competing suitors. Her heart skipped a beat, and it was all she could do to keep from running forward. The others waited politely and pointedly until she reached them and then all proceeded with much decorum to the judge's chambers.

The whole town had been aware of Ms. Dubarry's wealth. How extensive it was however, no one could even begin to fathom. Her father, and two uncles had been bankers in New Orleans, and later became heavily invested in land. Sugar cane, and cotton had then contributed substantially to the vast fortune. Ms. Dubarry's aunt had married and settled just outside of Elk Grove. When Ms. Dubarry was young, she was extremely fond of her aunt and would come to visit her a great deal, and at the death of her father had come to stay with her permanently. As a young girl, she had also developed an interest in wax sculpting. It was on a trip to Europe that she had taken with her father that she became introduced to such an odd thing. She became fascinated with the figures she had seen and wanted to form her own. Her father had indulged her and imported a capable Frenchman to tutor her in the subject. Her father not only imported the Frenchman, but also his immediate family. This family was given a couple of house servants to help with the duties. These servants were a husband and wife, who then had two children, Esther and Morris. Esther and Morris were taught to help with all aspects of wax-sculpting, and were also taught to record all expenditures for the hobby of the girl. This, however, did not take place until the young girl became a young woman. Only for a short time did the young lady lose interest in the wax figures she had created. This was when she had married her first husband. He had abhorred the hobby, and had forbid her having anything whatsoever to do with it. Martha, being very much in love, obediently warehoused her me-

A Blind Eye, a Missing Appendage, and a Friendly Card Game

nagerie at her aunt's place. It was then that she started to drink. She had no other hobbies than creating wax sculptures and when not allowed to create them outright, she would try and drown the desire out of her mind by drink. Later, her husband succumbed to an outbreak of disease and passed on. It was only out of respect for his hatred of the wax sculptures that she didn't create one of him. However, at his death, she had felt a freedom that she had never felt before. Along with dusting off the old sculptures, she created a whole new set. Her hobby became so widely known that people from all over would come to view her sculptures. She had inherited, by this time, Morris and Esther, who knew the business well. This was good, as she had not given up the drink, and they could help her when she became too inebriated to work. They would help her to bed, tucking her in, and would look after her and the many wax figures. They would escort people through the building that had been built, adjoining the house, when Martha was "under the weather." It was Morris who began insisting that it would be a good idea to charge a small fee for the tour. Ms. Dubarry would prop herself up to collect fees at the door, when she couldn't give the tours herself. Esther would keep watch and when Martha would be at the point of falling out of her chair, she would then take over collecting the fees. The best time seemed to be at night when they could light lanterns in the darkness, which lent an eerie life-like quality to the figures. People came from miles around to view the "museum." Morris soon took over the books for the whole household, the entire estate left by her now dead aunts and uncles. Martha Dubarry was a very wealthy woman, indeed. And when there were rumors of war, and talk that the north might blockade the southern ports, thereby suspending all trade in cotton from the south to Europe, Morris, upon Ms Dubarry's authorized signature, had a good bit of the holdings transferred to European banks.

After looking over the books of Ms. Dubarry's holdings, the judge became convinced, along with Ms. Dubarry's own counsel, that all was not only in order, but that all of her wealth was looked after with the greatest of care by Morris and Esther. Not

A Blind Eye, a Missing Appendage, and a Friendly Card Game

only her wealth, but also Ms. Dubarry, herself. She was well taken care of, and had prospered tremendously over the past few years. Not only had she prospered in the past, but by all indications, she would continue to do so. This, in spite of the influence of alcohol. Now, whether she in some instances made decisions on her own is not known. It was speculated that she must have at times. Her sobriety during the trial at least indicated her awareness of what was going on.

The biggest problem, however, had been with testimony of a certain Corporal Witherington. He had turned up just at the most inopportune moment, earlier in the week, when the judge was going to rule without question that Ms. Dubarry was completely, and totally competent. What Corporal Witherington had to say was what caused a great sensation throughout town and the whole of the countryside.

It was enough that negroes were actually running Ms. Dubarry's affairs. The whole town wasn't aware of this, just a few. What became a great sensation was the question of what had transpired when Corporal Witherington had done some labor for the household. Hired to paint the house, and the buildings (now two) which housed the sculptures, he swore that during that time the most atrocious happenings transpired. He swore, incredible as it may sound, that that was how he had even lost his leg.

The whole town was astonished to find out, as presented in the testimony of Corporal Witherington, the fantastic goings-on behind the doors of the house proper of Ms. Dubarry. He swore, under oath, that he had been invited in to dinner, only to have been drugged, and that the three inhabitants had dined upon him. To the whole of the courtroom, now transfixed by his testimony, Mr. Witherington asserted that he was "lucky to have escaped with just having lost a leg."

The newspapers, realizing a great opportunity to sell papers, had come up with a perfect drawing. This drawing showed two elegantly dressed Negroes, obviously Morris and Esther, poised with upraised knife and fork, looking with delectable delight over the body of Corporal Witherington as he lay serenely on the dining table. The two sat on opposite sides of the table, while at the head, looking

A Blind Eye, a Missing Appendage, and a Friendly Card Game

menacingly down at the face of the victim, or victuals in this case, was the very unflattering portrait of Ms. Martha Dubarry. She was depicted as a hag of a witch, hair teased outward from her head, a mole upon her nose, and a perceived cackle upon her open lips. Her smile, sans tooth, of course, was also poised in half-starved delight.

Not only was the scene itself appalling, but the newspaper went on to suggest that the wax figures came alive after dark and partook of the leftovers. They stirred the town's collective imagination, and even those who were appalled, insisted on buying a copy to see the picture and read the story. The newspaper sold out within an hour, and had to print five more runs. The courtroom became completely packed after this.

The defense became immediately, understandably obsessed with finding out what really happened to Corporal Witherington's appendage. He was not a local, but had merely been passing through town. Whether he had deserted his army and the great cause, or whether he had just been on furlough, it was not known. Eventually, his regiment was traced and the surgeon who had removed his leg contacted. Though the surgeon could not come and testify, he sent one of the men of the regiment with a letter to certify his statement, and as having been a witness to the appendage's removal, the letter carrier did testify. The rest of Corporal Witherington did then disappear very quickly, one would assume upon his own volition, and not at the hands of Ms. Dubarry and her servants as they were being closely watched by the townspeople at this point.

All of this transpired, but not before, under cover of darkness, some person or persons, presumably teenagers, by breaking a window, had made way into one of the buildings that housed the wax sculptures and absconded with the figure of Napoleon. He could not have more stealthily escaped the isle of Elba, as he disappeared under the watchful gaze of the respectable George Washington. Several other Revolutionary figures were present. Ben Franklin, who then stood, as he now stands with handkerchief in hand. More current figures exist, such as the General Ms. Dubarry had recently started.

A Blind Eye, a Missing Appendage, and a Friendly Card Game

She works only when she isn't too drunk to cause damage. Her hands are deft and practiced, and there is the watchful presence of Morris to guide her. He affixes the glass eyes very carefully, and forms the molds. Esther sews the clothing, and does a fine job. There is nothing sinister about the wax figures, nothing like the newspaper reports. This General, too current for her to decide if she should complete him. Should she complete him, and then should he lose the war, she would have to hide him or re-mold him into something else. And so, he stands, half-finished for now. Replicas of several prominent townspeople are present in the warehouse also, including the judge who is to decide her fate. Other examples of those she saw in Europe are in the building.

The wax model replica of David's *Death of Marat*, was set aflame by those who broke in, which was understandable to most of the townspeople, as his odious pose bespoke of unaccountable horrors, but mostly, at least in their minds, because he is shown in the bath, and to be shown dead in the bath is somehow too much for them. Some sane citizens, passing by, however, dragged the flaming sculpture out of the building, thus saving the rest of the pieces. It seemed amazing to those who were present at the flaming man in the bath, that he wasn't screaming horribly and writhing as the flames licked up and about him into the darkness. After being doused with water, he was blackened, and half melted. In the morning, he resembled a slave that had been recaptured and tortured by his owner.

By the end of the trial, the judge had had enough. He called a recess, opting for a short period of deliberation, and stated that he would give a verdict in the morning. Needing to clear his mind of all the crazy events, the 'nonsense' of the trial during the previous week, he decided there would be no better way than to have the usual friendly game of cards with his usual partners. One of the players was the town doctor, and then there was the local merchant, and a couple well known and highly respected people of Elk Grove who shall remain nameless. The pastor declined to accept the invitation to play because he had to hold a special prayer meeting to combat whatever evil doings that may have been ex-

A Blind Eye, a Missing Appendage, and a Friendly Card Game

cited or evoked in the minds of the townspeople due to the newspaper and the testimony of the Corporal, and due the trial in general. Other players included counsel for the defense and of course, the prosecutor. These were all amicable, well respected men, just having a friendly game of cards. It was inevitable that the counsel for the defense accept a small token of encouragement from Ms. Martha Dubarry, delivered by the venerable Morris. Though no one can specify the exact amount that this token of encouragement and appreciation was, it was speculated to not be so small a token to insult anyone, or hurt anyone's feelings. And it was inevitable that the judge win a few good hands, in which a substantial bit of this token was placed in the pot. All participants seemed pleased with the outcome of the friendly card game.

And so, the question of Ms. Dubarry's competence became the question of what actually happened to the missing appendage of Corporal Witherington. The question of the missing appendage being solved, which then led to his whole body disappearing, thankfully (at least to the town of Elk Grove), and finally to a friendly card game the night before the verdict which put the whole case to rest.

Everyone seemed relieved, none more so than Ms. Dubarry, as she raised her glass in a toast to the judge, in all of his veritable, even if somewhat myopic, wisdom.

He blushed and did not begrudge the small, elderly lady's request to partake of a cigar along with the rest. Who can question, or deny such a request from a lady who has had to recently suffer such outrageous, and heinous accusations of –BANG!

The shot reverberated through the building, startling the small party to no small degree. It had come from the direction of the courtroom. Everyone rushed immediately to the scene, the bailiff in the lead. He moved with tremendous agility, scaling the benches and running across most of the seating in the room, much as a man would run across hot coals. He tackled Deputy Cosgrove to the floor and wrested the gun from his hands. All eyes then went to Morris Garvin, who lie wounded and bleeding,

A Blind Eye, a Missing Appendage, and a Friendly Card Game

with Esther leaning over him. It was soon determined to be a mere flesh wound, however, and Esther had not been hurt at all.

There did not need to be a trial in Cosgrove's case. The local council wisely decided to run him out of town on rails, quietly, in the dead of night. On the night of the endeavor, Cosgrove was led into the darkness by two men, the bailiff being one, the other remaining nameless. The moon, with judicious refrain, remained under cover of clouds long enough to lend just the proper touch of respectability.

Only Those Most Deserving

A thought can be a dangerous thing if a man clings too tightly to it. I guess it's much like a horse's saddle being cinched too close. He can and probably will throw you, sure as I'm talkin' right now. I don't know that that analogy is the most perfect one, but it's the only one coming to mind. But I suppose to Nate's way of thinkin' a thought can be a man's salvation, dangerous or not. And religion, well . . . most men take to it okay and nuthin' much is made of it. But any thought can cause a man to do strange things if he focuses on a thing in the wrong way. . . Let me just explain instead of just ramblin' on like I am.

Nate, well he had seen a lot during the war; We all had. But Nate had seen the results at Ft. Pillow. I ain't judging whether all those black men deserved to die like they did, any more than any white man. That ain't my contention. The war was fought for a lot of different reasons and each man had his own. My reason I reckon was fairly general, probably like most of the men fightin.'

I had known Nate a good while I suppose before he found religion, and I can't really recall whether it was a gradual thing or somethin' that just happened overnight. All I remember is being in the midst of battle and him askin' me in an offhand way which one of the rebs across from us I thought was most deserving. And he asked it more than once.

He'd have a certain glint in his eye and he would ask it in between the volleys.

"Clarence," he'd say.

I would be tryin' to concentrate on my aim, and just tryin' to watch my own rear, not intendin' to be deserving in any way myself. And I reckon' anyone who wasn't attending to what was happening around him when it came to fightin' might just be the most deserving fellow there could be. So, half the time I wouldn't pay him much of a mind and he would keep on pestering me until I responded.

"Clarence," he'd call out again. "Which one of those Rebs do you reckon is most deserving?'"

One particular time we both just narrowly dodged behind two adjacent trees as he called out. It was a hot afternoon, in a beautiful area of woods with just enough of a clearing that I reckon some poor sap of a farmer had tried farming before the war came along and his land became a battlefield. I had just been wondering why we had to be fightin' on such a beautiful day, at such a beautiful place. It all seemed strange to me that we should be shootin' at each other at all. I couldn't at that moment even contemplate on the subject. I was particularly irritated. Betwixt the heat and him chatterin' away like he was . . .

"Hell, Nate," I responded. "Can't you just for once shut up with your damn silly questions and just fire."

I think I caught him a little off guard, and I didn't really mean to, but like I said, I was particularly irritated that afternoon.

He was silent for a long minute, and he wasn't firing at anything either. I looked over at him then and he didn't seem bothered too terribly much about it. He just looked at me underneath his flop of reddish-brown hair. It pretty much covered his right eye, where his head was tilted forward, and he was looking at me in a calm manner, just smirking.

I didn't give it much thought then and there, at least not on a conscious level. It was only later, much later that I thought about it. We all did later, when it was too late. That strange afternoon, though, shootin' out across that field, that's when I should have noticed it. It's always easier to see afterwards though. Always.

That night, or the next one, I'm not exactly sure . . . was when we were casually sitting around the camp, relaxed and feeling somewhat safe, not to mention a little more sane. The night was comforta-

Only Those Most Deserving

bly cool and the fire was burning down, the embers glinting and flickering, almost like it was winking and smiling up at us. We'd had a little bit of grub, and that helped the mood. That was the next time Nate posed the question to me. But he did it in a much different way then.

"Forget the Rebs," he started. There was a slight pause before he continued. "Which one of us do you reckon is most deserving?"

"Most deserving?" I asked it with a blank, mildly questioning look, as though it was the first time I had heard the question.

"Yeah, Clarence. Right here. Right here in this regiment. Which one of us is most deserving of everlasting life?"

"Ever--"

"And I don't mean here on earth, either. I mean in heaven."

"Hm." I watched Anderson get up and walk off from us. I'm not sure how much of it he was paying attention to anyways. He disappeared into the darkness.

"Well? Which one?"

"Me, of course." I grinned.

"That right there is a prideful man talking. And a prideful man ain't deserving at all."

"Well, you asked."

"I'm serious, Clarence, now. Give it to me straight."

"Okay, well . . . let's see . . . how about Darius?"

"He gambles."

"Yeah, he does. Not too often, but he does play on occasion though. Not like Reeves, but he does, you're right."

"So, he's out."

"Agreed, but he would be a close runner, if'n there ever was one."

"Think harder."

"Okay, how about Sheffield?"

"Perfect," Nate said, after giving it some thought. "Sheffield is truly deserving.

"I – He just popped into my mind," I said. "But he is . . . he's perfect. I can't think of anyone more deserving."

We sat in silence for a little while, both pleased with our pick. Looking back now I can see Nate's eyes aglow in the firelight. The flames flickering in the darkness. We both were comfortable playing this little game. It took our thoughts away from the fighting for a few minutes.

"I can't think of anyone else," I said after a couple of minutes.

"There are a couple of others. How about Jameson?"

"Right. I agree. Jameson's a good candidate, in love with his girl back home, doesn't go whoring, doesn't gamble. He's pretty straight-up."

We sat in silence again. My mind left the little game we were playing and wandered all over the place, mainly back home. I thought of several different girls. Finally, I wanted to be alone with my thoughts. I stood up. "Well," I said. "I'm gonna turn in for the night."

I patted him on the shoulder as I passed him. "See you in the mornin' buddy."

"See you," he mumbled. He didn't really glance up, or if he did his patch of unruly hair hung low and blocked it, but I could swear I saw his eyes still flickering as he stared into the fire, lost in thought.

It was a week later we all woke to find Sheffield dead. He'd had his throat slit in the night. The killing had been done quietly and efficiently. Everyone wondered how the enemy had snuck in and murdered one of our men. Everyone suspected Smith of falling asleep at his post. Several said as much out loud. Everyone was a bit jumpy after that. Days passed along, however, bringing the war with it. We fought it out in the daylight and didn't think too much more about it. Death was death, however it came. We lost a few in the fighting. Sheffield was one among the many. We buried him and went on about business.

It really wasn't until much later that I realized Nate had stopped asking me which reb was most deserving. It had always been the question, always in the midst of battle. And then it just stopped coming. I didn't think much about it.

A month or so later Anderson found Jameson, same as Sheffield, throat slit pretty-as-you-please. We all just stood in the dawn's early light, looking down at him. He was lying peacefully, still in his bedding, but with an extra smile under his chin.

Only Those Most Deserving

I glanced at Nate. He appeared stunned, looking like everyone else. That's when it sort of hit me, just an itch, or an inkling of an idea. Okay, I confess, it was more than an inkling after a second or two. It sprang to mind like a volley of grapeshot spattering an open field around me. It propelled me into action. I had to wait a couple of days at least to let things become calm.

A day or so later I pulled Anderson aside and filled him in on things. I wasn't sure he was going to believe me. I don't really know how much of the conversation he had heard that night around the fire. He had left at the very beginning of it all, but perhaps he had heard enough.

Everyone had been jumpy after Sheffield's death, but now it was like popping corn over a fire. It couldn't happen again. It's a wonder the Captain hadn't ordered a firing squad out for Smith.

After two weeks or so of nothing happening, at least no in-camp murders, things began to calm, not much, but enough. And again we were sitting around the fire. The battlefield had been calm that day. There had been some skirmishing, but not like it had been. Perhaps everyone was simply too hot and tired, to go on fighting without a little rest. After a little while it was just Nate and I. I tried to prod him into the same conversation we had had before, regarding who would be most deserving. I had to be careful, approach it casually.

"So, Nate," I said. "I've been thinking . . ."

He looked over at me.

"I can't seem to think of anybody who is most deserving."

He looked at me for a long second or two. A hint of something sprang into his eyes for just a second. Fear? Then the edges of his lips curled up into a slightly nervous smile, just for a second and then went back down. Was it my imagination? He wouldn't look at me after that. He sat still, continued looking at the fire.

"Yep, I figure I've gone over all the fellows pretty thorough-like. I simply can't come up with a single one who would be deserving." I waited a minute or so longer. Then just long enough.

I continued prodding. "Except maybe Smith."

Nate continued looking into the fire.

"He sure is getting persecuted. You think he really fell asleep on watch?"

Nate just shrugged in response, kept staring at the flames.

I pushed it some more. I had to plant the seed.

"I wonder if he saw anything? Maybe he's just afraid to speak out."

Nate didn't say anything.

"Nah, probably not," I continued. "He's an upstanding fellow, but he has been known to fall asleep on watch though." Still nothing from Nate.

After a few minutes I went and turned in.

It was two nights later that Nate was caught. Smith wasn't sleeping much these days, on watch or not. He jumped up when Nate was coming toward him. There was a struggle, and then a man named Ellis jumped in to help Smith.

That very next morning, shortly after daybreak, the Captain ordered a firing squad. Funny thing though; The firing squad never got the chance. The Captain was so furious, and so determined that no one should say a prayer for Nate. He didn't seem to even want to allow time for Nate to have the opportunity to pray for himself. He surprised everyone with his anger. He was so furious with Nate and religion in general that he didn't even give the firing squad time to fire. The whole thing went something akin to this:

"So, you think you're deserving?" the Captain said. He especially, and in a very derisive manner put the emphasis on the word 'deserving'. He glared at Nate as he said it.

Nate swallowed hard, but then gathered himself up bravely to face down the Captain. He only stuttered for a second. "Ye—yessir, I do."

The Captain glared some more and I actually began to feel sorry for Nate.

The Captain raised his arm, his revolver pointed at Nate's temple. "Ready . . ." The Captain said this out of the corner of his mouth, but it was loud and authoritative, in the direction of the squad of men.

The firing squad raised their arms. It was almost as though they were forgetting the Captain was standing in the line of fire. They seemed to be just automatically following orders. The Captain seemed to trust in the men not to fire before ordered. He asked Nate another question with his sidearm still aimed directly at Nate's temple. "Tell me, son, which direction you believe you'll be headed."

Nate appeared puzzled at first, but then uttered his response. "Why, Heaven, Sir – If the good Lord be will--"

And with that the Captain fired directly into the boy's head.

It was then that I muttered a prayer for Nate. I was careful to utter it only under my breath and this in spite of orders. I'm sure that several of the other men did the same. I'm sure that several of the firing party were relieved that the burden of killing Nate was lifted from them. And it was then that I realized I might have made a mistake.

Had I realized that Nate would handle his death so gracefully and calmly, this would have moved him into the spot of being absolutely *the most deserving* of all of us, and I would have killed him first instead of Sheffield. But then again, things probably wouldn't have turned out quite so beautifully. And I'm sure all three of them made it into heaven. And, well, though I resented the Captain for being so cruel, I do realize that he had a job to do. Perhaps he knew what he was doing, saving the other men from having to kill a fellow soldier. Though they all were under the impression that Nate was guilty, some of them still would have had trouble killing him. They might not have realized this until after the fact, however. They would have been haunted by this incident, haunted long after the war...

And so, you see what I mean about thoughts being dangerous if one holds onto one too tightly? Had it not been for that day of fighting in that beautiful field, . . . that day I especially desired not to be fighting, the day that, once again, Nate asked the damn fool question about which Reb would be most deserving . . . that day--That was the day the notion struck me that there was no way in hell I could determine which Reb was 'deserving,' but I could very well determine which one of my own side was most deserving to enter the "life everlasting." And each one could do so by my own hand, more peacefully than at the hands of the enemy. And by ending each of these most deserving lives before each one committed another murder of another man, which would lessen his own deservedness.

Only Those Most Deserving

Yes, that day, on that very field, that question suddenly struck me. Nate had asked it a million times before, but that was the day the thought entered my mind like a lizard scurrying under a rock or into some dark crevice in the side of a hill. I might not have acted, however, had the train of thought not been pursued the night around the fire. It was Nate who led me to it. It had struck me that day on the field, and then he alone, almost as though he had read my mind, pursued the line and solidified the thought. I was like a bug trapped in ice. That ice didn't thaw until much later, long after the war.

However, and I say this in all honesty, I do take sole responsibility for my actions. It was I who maneuvered Nate to approach Smith that night, telling him that Anderson wanted to be relieved from watch so that he could relieve himself, and that I also had eaten something upsetting to me and had to do the same, precluding me from going on to deliver the message to Smith. I had convinced Nate that it would be Smith's chance to redeem himself, and that he should convince Smith of this. And so, events played out as such. Nate was never allowed the chance to explain, or proclaim his own innocence. Though, I confess, it all could have backfired. The thought was absolutely dangerous, and so too, were the actions that followed it. But I felt at the time that I did what needed to be done. The whole thing consumed me then and there, in that span of time.

And then the ice started to melt, or to go back to the earlier analogy, the cinch was loosened. The thought seemed to let go of me some then, only lingering in the back of my mind. And the war went on and eventually ended. I was not killed in combat, as I should have been. In spite of my jesting with Nate about my being the most deserving. I honestly did not then, nor do I now believe that I am worthy or deserving of anything except that which the good Lord decides to mete out to me on judgment day. Perhaps it does make me a prideful man indeed, for feeling that I did those boys a favor. I honestly did believe that those boys were the most deserving. And I still believe it.

Daguerreotype Dreams

Avery Howard Johnson sat on the edge of his bed. He felt the jar in his hand warming as it filled. It had taken him a little time to get the stream going, but now it was going strong – at least until the knock on the door sounded. Then Avery just sat looking down and frowning. He wasn't quite sure what to do. He looked hesitantly up at the door, staring for a minute, waiting. He looked back down. He sat teetering between two thoughts: Was he awake? Was he asleep? A third thought now wedged its way into his mind and nestled right between the other two: Who was at the door?

His was a frazzled mind, a battleground of sorts; had been for months now. Had there been enough light in the room one could see the dark circles around his eyes. The wrinkles and lines. The harried look. His hair stood out in odd points and conical shapes, pointing away from his head. If there was just a small dim light, one might think him a court jester of olden times by these shapes sticking out from his head, as though he had bells attached to the ends of the odd points. There was no light, nor bells, just the knock at the door. It sounded again.

Looking back down, he thought, no use. He moved slowly, carefully, setting the jar on the wooden plank floor by the bed. Quiet. He waited. Maybe they'll go away?

"I can't," he muttered to himself. Just a slight, soft murmur, barely any air crossed his lips. Maybe it was no more than another thought, this one racing across his mind, frantic, looking for a place to hide. Avery trembled. He wanted to follow it. It was a solid thought, the first solid thought he had had in months. He wanted to chase after it, follow it into some dark, safe, hiding-place. Avery's left arm twitched involuntarily, as though some force inside of him could propel it up and into his head to grasp the thought. He looked at his arm, his hand. He could almost make them out in the darkness. The thought was now long-gone. He couldn't even remember what it was. Was it his salvation? Whatever it was, it was no more . . .

The knock sounded again. Not insistent. Not impatient.

Avery hadn't opened his door now for quite some time. Had it been months? A year? Oh, not true. He had in fact opened it. Each time the boy came by to deliver food. After he was sure the boy had gone. Then. Only then would he open the door. And he would look down and away. He hadn't looked at another human being for at least a year now. He couldn't. It was unbearable. He would simply slide a coin out for the boy and shut the door, listening for his footsteps, his return. There might even be a slight scrape of the coin on the wooden step as the boy picked it up. That was all. And not every time.

"Oh—twins," he had said. "And so lovely too!"

The couple looked at him, horrified. They took their daughter by the hand and led her away. They were moving quickly, not looking back. The little girl looked back, once, just once, a smile playing across her lips.

Avery hadn't understood then, not at all, but that was the first time it happened. How could he have understood? His only thought then was an afterthought. What happened to the little girl who had been dancing around the one now being led away? What happened to the twin? He heard a faint giggling sound in the distance, not so distant really, somewhere near . . .

It was only later, a month or so later, that he found out what had happened to the girl's twin. He had been in town for some reason or another and had spotted the mother and the little girl. Another woman saw him looking and leaned in toward him. "It's so awful what happened." He looked at the woman. He was puzzled. He noticed that she was looking at the woman and child.

"What?" he asked.

The woman who had spoken looked at him. She searched his face and noted that his inquiry seemed sincere.

"What? He said again. "What happened?"

The woman still almost scoffed, still unsure. Her gaze then moved to where the woman and child had been. Her mouth hung open for a moment, silent. And then she spoke. "Why, her twin fell down a well and died. Going on two years now." She stood silent again and then added, something, somewhat as an afterthought. "Such beautiful little girls, too. A pretty little pair they made."

Avery had stood still, perplexed. He glanced to the same space the woman and child had been a couple of moments before. He started to turn back to the woman he had been speaking with, but something caught his eye, just as he turned, a flicker. Just for a brief instant, a split second, out of the corner of his eye he thought he saw something. The girl's twin, smiling at him, giggling silently to herself, laughing at him, mocking him.

For weeks afterward she haunted his dreams. He would see her small body lying at the bottom of a well, her little cheek pressed into the mud and muck of the semi dry well, her neck broken, her body twisted in a weird fashion. Her eye, the one he could see in his dreams was open and staring, wide. He looked to where she gazed. A beetle was crawling up the wall, just inches from the bottom. It fell, landing on its back, tiny legs twitching and wiggling in the air. Eventually it righted itself again, and once again moved over to the wall, again attempting to climb. In his dreams Avery would look back at where the little girl lay. She still watched, her eye wide open, forever. The repetitiveness on the beetle's part was maddening, over and over again . . .

That was the first time it happened. And something was out of sync then. It was different than the times that followed. That was the only time the person, the subject of the daguerreotype had been deceased *before* they sat for him. Or, rather, before the relatives or loved-ones sat for him. From then on, though not right away, and not always – at least not at first, the person who sat for him would be the person to appear in his mind. Just for a moment would they appear to him. His head would be under

Daguerreotype Dreams

the hood. And there they would be, but that moment would be the moment of, or just after death. That would be the image that he would see. The flash, the death image, the smoke. And there would be a sharp, tangy taste of metal in his mouth. He never really thought about it before, the order, but that was it. And the daguerreotype would be forever etched upon his mind.

Only occasionally now would he dream about the girl. And on rare occasions her body would just be floating in the well, the water there, at least a few feet of it.

And the dreams, well . . .

Every person he had taken a daguerreotype of would be there, only it would be the death mask, so to speak, of them. It would be the etched plate of what he saw, and what he had witnessed, death! And he would not just see one plate, but all of them. All the plates would be lined up, one behind the other, and they would fall forward, one after another in rapid succession. He knew they were his plates because they would have his initials in them, bottom right corner: AHJ.

And so even the ones he had forgotten about would be shown to him, and there would be a rattling of the plates. Much like when they were still blank and being transported to the battlefield during the war. And the soldiers he had captured would be there, all of them, dead, eyes staring at nothing. No repetitive beetle for them to watch, nothing.

Oh, he would remember some of them, okay, most of them, but some stood out, lingered in his dreams. For instance, the young boy he saw hanged. That was all he saw, just the flash, the frame, the smoke. Oh, and the taste of metal. And in the young boy's case there was sound, the creak of the rope rubbing on the tree branch as he swung, gently, dangling. And in this case, at least most times that it played in his mind, he couldn't see the boy's face. He would just see the feet and legs, but somehow, he would know it was the boy. For a split second he would see the boy posing, a smile on his lips, and then the legs dangling, the sound of the rope rubbing the branch on a warm, breezy afternoon. And then there would be the smell of copper, almost a taste, in the air, in his nostrils. It was just as he had experienced back in his boyhood. He distinctly remembered the Daguerreotype process from when he had been a ten-year-old apprentice. The process was much different then, than the collodion-smeared glass process of today. And yet, it all seemed to be mixed in his dreams, his mind. There was no respect for, or delineation of time or process.

And there were more, so many, many more, between the girl and the boy, and then many more after the boy. All the way until he quit the business. And that didn't even stop the images. They haunted him day and night. They terrified him. If he looked at one more person and saw that person's death, he would go mad. But then, well . . . he was mad in any case. He closed himself off from the world, refusing to look upon another living human being. And then the thought hit him that he might even witness his own death if he saw his image in the looking glass. And, so he had turned it to the wall, shielding his face as he did so. He couldn't take the chance. He didn't want to take the chance after all – what would he see? Nothing perhaps. And yet there was that chance. He couldn't risk it. The thought terrified him, not as much as the dreams, or the visions of others. Only on some occasions did he get carried away and play the possibilities over and over again in his mind. The possibilities of when and how he would meet his demise were endless, and he would take that path sometimes, that maddening path of endless possibilities. Different scenarios would play over and over in his mind until he would be driven mad with curiosity, almost to the point of racing to the mirror and flinging it around to face it, to face himself, his death. At these times he would stand up from the bed and shoot directly over to the glass, ready to whip it around, his hand reaching out. And then another thought would hit him, the vision of him losing his grip on the thing as he turned it and it shattering to pieces on the floor, or perhaps against the wall. The possibilities were endless, but they would all be unknown to him then. He would not have access to the knowledge of his own death if the mirror broke. And with that thought he would be convinced he held a certain power, a power that other men did not hold. Was it not a powerful thing? To have the opportunity to view and know death so intimately, to know the cause and perhaps figure out the time – yes, yes, one could search for

Daguerreotype Dreams

clues in the evidence. There would be the appearance, which would indicate age, roughly. And with that there would often be clues as to the cause, like the boy dangling. He didn't know what the boy did, however, to come to such an end. But in other cases, things were obvious.

A specific memory then flashed into his mind. He had taken a daguerreotype (as he liked to refer to all of them now) of a young couple on their wedding day. That's when he saw the woman's death. She had apparently died in childbirth. She was lying still upon the bed, her face was contorted, yes, and hands were pulling a woolen blanket up over her face. Other things were happening, other indicators, indications of life. Arms, hands, holding a newborn child, handing it to the father, the husband.

Yes, yes . . . signs, signs of life . . . so it wasn't all death . . .

Or had he imagined the baby being alive, the life, the other movement? Perhaps his mind was playing tricks on him. There had been the times that he had been mad enough to believe that it had all just been his mind playing tricks. The whole time, just tricks.

The whole of death might merely have been his mind. These were the times he wanted to run and fling the door open. He wanted to rush out into the street, the world, just to check. All he had to do was uncover the window of his room and look out, or better yet, just fling the door wide . . .

Another knock sounded. The opportune moment. Rise, Rise! Open the door!

Avery Howard Johnson rose from the bed, stumbled across the jar, spilling it. He marched across to the door and – and stopped. Fear rode him, through him. It pounced upon him and arrested all further movement. His hand was on the door latch. A certain calmness hit him then. Perhaps it was all in his mind, the knock even. Perhaps it was all fantasy. Perhaps –

The knock sounded again. He jumped at the sound, startled. It was the same knock as before, not rushed, not loud, just a firm, patient knock. The door was unlatched now. Avery's hand rose, slowly. He heard the coin of the food boy scrape on the wood, not a momentary scrape but a long scraping sound, drawn out, a back and forth scraping sound. Perhaps – but no. It was then he heard the muffled laughter of a small child, a little girl, and he saw her. He saw her lying in the bottom of a well, one eye staring, a beetle repeatedly climbing, falling back, climbing again. Over and over. And it was too late. His hand rose, the door opened. He thought he heard footsteps then, running away, more laughter. Ah, he thought, a prank. But a hand reached out and down from the back of a horse. It gripped his wrist. And he had no feeling of its firm grasp. He went up easily. He couldn't see the rider's face. He could only see the little girl's face, her lying in the well bottom. There was a flash, an image, a puff of smoke. There was the smell, the taste of metal. And the image was of a man, a frightened, trembling, very tired man. The man was clinging desperately to the dark figure of a rider as the horse lunged off into the darkness of the night. The image was of a very terrified man, looking back over his shoulder, facing the doorway, longing to be safe within his room, safe in bed. And the initials etched into the daguerreotype's lower right corner, or the glass plate: A. H. J. And Avery heard this plate jar and rattle against all the others lined up; He knew not whether there was any certain order to them. He glanced up to the top of the plate, saw the fingers of the hand placing the plate with the others. The fingers seemed long and thin, with long dirty nails. Another image appeared in his mind's eye. Those fingers grasping a coin and scraping it across the boards of the porch. The rasping, grating sound of it, the sound that made him think it was the grocery boy returned. The sound that fooled him into opening the door. If he had turned the mirror around would he have seen it all ahead of time? Would the image in the mirror have forewarned him? His thoughts were interrupted as the sound of the plates rattled again. And he felt the jolt of the horse lunging forward. It lurched, spurred on by its cloaked rider. Avery gripped the cloak and held on tightly, still looking longingly back toward the open door. A singed and coppery scent filled his nostrils; but there was something else, a putrid stench of rotting flesh and decay. The horse lunged again, this time as though off a cliff. The animal boldly plunged, swift and steadfast, and with a sense of urgency, into darkness.

A Challenge

While a dinner party during wartime is always a challenge, somehow Washington High society always manages to pull it off, and the same can be said for New York, and Philadelphia as well. Early on in the war, in 1861, the parties were still in full swing, if not for the sole purpose of gathering or ferreting out intelligence on either side, then at least serving as forums, more or less, for high-spirited debate.

Mark Stattelman

There was a certain party, the hosts of which must remain nameless, or perhaps we could call them Mr. and Mrs. J. just for the sake of attaching names. For that matter, we can thinly disguise the two most prominent guests, or rather the ones who stand out most significantly in the story told, as Ms. Laura Foster, and Col. Samuel Rutherford, being that the two most prominent guests invited didn't show: that being the President and Mrs. Lincoln.

While Ms. Laura Foster was no slouch when it came to espionage, and a die-hard southern sympathizer, Col. Samuel Rutherford was an extremely competent intelligence gatherer for the Union, not to mention a highly effective interrogator of spies. Neither had met previously, yet each was acutely aware of the other's reputation. When the two were finally in the room together, even though each had yet to be introduced to the other, the atmosphere was almost alive, electric one could say, or palpable. There was a certain anticipation on both sides of the yet-to-occur meeting. One can only speculate as to whether the host and hostess had deliberately not introduced the two, leaving it up to the devices of

A challenge

these particularly inventive and creative individuals to create the meeting themselves.

Once the dinner got started, the other guests seemed to relax and mix it up, so to speak, forgetting these two. But these two individuals would casually glance, one at the other, at odd times, each one trying to do so as the other looked away. These glances, however, eventually tripped over one another, by sheer virtue of the inevitability of a sort of predestined meeting. They were like two combatants, crossing swords, playfully and affably, challenging each other in a non-threatening way – each in anticipation of the eventual coming together. Perhaps foreplay would be too strong a word for it.

Laura was a dark-haired beauty with flashing dark eyes to match. She was quick-witted and playful on the one hand, but could upon an instant turn into a seductive, smoldering temptress. She could bring most men to their knees with a glance, and then slay them with an ice-cold glare that would turn them to into withering, wilting plants.

Samuel Rutherford was not the slickest, nor the cleverest person in the room, ever. And perhaps that was his strength. As Americans go, the general consensus seemed to be that if one were too slick and polished, one would be less inclined to be trusted. Sam was a plain-spoken man, somewhat stocky, handsome without being too pretty. His jaw was set in an honest and firm manner, and he managed to keep an open and inviting gaze. His gray eyes were unique in that they registered a non-threatening intelligence, one that often surprised those around him. His cheeks were slightly pudgy and his hairline was receding just a bit. He had a solidly light complexion. In essence, he was a man who fit the mold of his time.

In any case, the two managed to avoid looking at one another for the longest period of time of the evening. It was almost too much to withstand, but only after their glances had tripped repeatedly over one another. It finally became necessary, at least in Laura's eyes, to take action. She rose slowly from her seat, the gentlemen on either side of her each racing to be the first to pull out her chair as she stood. This caused a stir among the men's wives, and each man was reprimanded with a darkened glance from each respective wife. These men didn't

A challenge

notice, however, as they were then too busy watching Laura walk along the length of the table. There were a couple of smiles, and even a snicker or two about the table.

Laura seemed oblivious to the disturbance. She appeared to be going to speak to the hostess, as her eyes were trained in that direction, but at the last second, just as she arrived at Col. Rutledge's chair, something fluttered to the floor.

It was without thought, just an instinctive reaction for him to reach and retrieve her small cloth, a signal for the game to begin. She had gone two steps past him before he reached up and lightly touched her elbow. She turned, effortlessly, and he handed her the kerchief. She gave but the faintest smile as their eyes met, and then she turned away. It was only a half turn, however. She stopped and turned back. "Thank you," she said. "General, is it?" she asked. "General Rutledge?" She knew very well that it was Colonel, and an honorary title at that, and he knew that she knew. He almost turned crimson, but managed to arrest his emotion quickly enough. She knew, however, that her first thrust had drawn blood, just a little, but all the same the game was on, the challenge set. She walked on, her face turned away from him, only a slight smile of triumph danced across her lips, almost imperceptible. She proceeded to speak nonchalantly to the hostess. I would be giving too much away to say that the two had known each other since they were little girls, so pretend I never mentioned it.

Very soon the women withdrew to the parlor to chat, while the men stepped out onto the porch to enjoy cigars. The hired help cleared the now vacant dining table. The chandeliers glittered within, while the stars glittered without. The night was balmy, but the swamp of Washington proper was actually several blocks away, and the mosquitoes followed the breeze eastward, away from the house.

It was then, over cigars, while the other men spoke of the war that Col. Samuel Rutledge stood quietly smoking and forming his plan. He rolled the cigar across his lower lip, spit out a bit of the tobacco that had worked its way inside his mouth. When someone asked him a direct question about the war, he managed to have been paying enough attention to respond appropriately, and yet his mind was on

A challenge

Laura Foster, and just how he would trap her. A full and complete plan hadn't surfaced yet, but the first stages of it had quietly formed. After a second or so more of thought, he approached the host and requested that he might have a word with him. A couple of minutes later a servant was dispatched with a note, and within fifteen minutes or so a young man appeared at the side of the porch to confer with Col. Rutledge. When this man left, Samuel Rutledge turned his attention to the other guests. He seemed much more affable and very much at ease. The plan was put into motion. The night was still young, and all he had to do was wait to see how things played out. After a few more minutes the men returned to the inner comfort of the house. Several of the men gathered their wives and many of the couples left for the evening.

The Colonel lingered for a moment on the porch before entering the house. A cat jumped up on the porch railing and walked along it. Sam Rutledge stroked its back, just briefly, as it passed. It stopped for a second and peered up at him. It arched its back upward as he stroked it. It was a white feline with one dark patch just below its left eye.

The cat's eyes shone brightly, reflecting the inner lights of the house. Col. Rutledge could hear the sounds behind him of more guests leaving. The group, he imagined was becoming less formal, a more intimate circle, friends of the hosts. He hoped it wasn't becoming too intimate too quickly, or he would have to leave. He wasn't on that close of terms with anyone at the party. Perhaps he should have brought a date. His usual friend and sometimes companion, a girl named Jenny, was otherwise engaged for the evening. If things became too intimate and loose, he thought, he would simply have to leave. The thought disappointed him. Having met the notorious Laura Foster he wanted very much to pursue her, not in the sense that most men would, however. His pursuit was of a more professional nature. He had no doubt that she would be caught at some point in some sort of treachery, whether by himself or someone else. No one had, as of yet obviously done so, and he played with the thought of it being him. He shrugged and turned to enter the house and almost bumped directly into

A challenge

her as she was exiting the door. She had to stop immediately, raising her shoulders and arching her back to avoid the collision. He saw that she held a bottle of wine in one hand and two wine glasses in the other. This is why she had hunched her shoulders. She had abruptly pulled the items into her body, trying to protect them. Both of them, her and the Colonel, seemed startled. A small gasp escaped her lips, followed be a slight giggle. So, she was human, after all. He wondered suddenly, vaguely, why he had to remind himself of this . . . of course she was human. He scoffed inwardly. Instinctively, his guard went up, however.

Laura looked around, obviously for someone else. "Have you seen--" she started and then stopped. She looked up at him and smiled. "Oh well," she shrugged. "Would you like some wine?"

Col. Rutledge pulled out his watch and turned it toward the light from the doorway.

"Oh, certainly you can't have business to attend at this hour?"

He looked at her and smiled, his smile becoming instantly affable. Of course, he had business, he thought, her. And she knew there was a war going on, obviously. She also had business. He guessed her business had left the party early, having escaped her. And so now it was him. There was a sound from within the house, someone was calling out for him. He raised his eyebrows at her. "I guess I do," he said and went in. He wasn't far from the door when the man handed him the paper. He thanked the messenger. The messenger then did an about face and left. There was almost a salute in there. He wondered if she had seen it from the doorway. Something for her to harass him about. He resisted the urge to turn and see if she was watching. He studied the document momentarily, re-folded it and stuck it in his pocket. He then turned and headed back toward the door leading to the porch. He took note of the fact that she was standing just inside the door speaking with the hostess of the house. He glanced around. There seemed to be several couples and a few other intimate conversations going on. One man was passed out in a chair. He wondered if that had been the man for whom she had been searching on the porch. He looked back at her. She seemed even more relaxed than he had at first perceived. She was

A challenge

indeed a very beautiful woman. He reminded himself just how dangerous she could be. He thought of lives lost due to information she had acquired and passed on to other southern sympathizers, those who smuggled such information across enemy lines. He wasn't personally aware that she had ever crossed the lines herself. He decided that she could have done so easily enough, but that she was probably much more valuable to the southern cause in Washington. She knew all the right people and could maneuver easily enough around its environs. She glanced at him and smiled as he approached. It was an inviting smile, friendly. He noticed then that the bottle of wine was still unopened.

"Business concluded," he said. "Now, shall we open this?" He casually lifted the bottle out of her hands. She seemed a little surprised at his abrupt change, but she took it in stride and smiled at the hostess before following the Colonel out onto the porch. He had the bottle uncorked and ready to pour when she came out with the glasses.

The sun was well up in the sky when Col. Sam Rutledge woke. At first, he had trouble comprehending where he was. He was lying face down on the veranda of the home where he had gone to the dinner party. Drool hung from his lips and strung out onto the wooden porch. He rose up and looked around. Over the porch railing he saw a puddle of vomit. His head ached with an incredible intensity. The sunlight was excruciating. His mouth was dry. His jacket lay across the porch swing. Slowly, among the images that gradually, slowly filtered into his mind, he made out the smiling face of Laura Foster. Then he remembered other things. He distinctly remembered the messenger coming to the host's home and delivering the documents to him. He checked his pockets, searched all of them, empty. Oh, he still had all of his personal items, cash, etc. What was missing were the documents, the false documents. He then smiled with relief. She had fallen for it. She had in fact seen the messenger hand him the documents, just as he had hoped. He had her. She might have gotten the better of him with the wine, but she wouldn't escape his grasp in the long run. He sat on the swing and sighed. He

A challenge

rubbed his face. God, he wanted to be home in bed. He couldn't though. There was still too much to do. Perhaps he could just sit here and gather himself for a few minutes. How had she done it? He was no lightweight when it came to drink. There had to have been something more, something added to the drink, some sort of opiate or another. Laudanum? He had watched her closely. She had just as carefully watched him. Neither had gotten close to the other's glass as far as he was aware. Always there had been new bottles opened. God, how many? Four? No, couldn't have been. Three at least though. Yes, he was sure of it. She had gone and gotten the cellar key from the host. Perhaps she had simply snuck into the room and swiped it. He wasn't sure. How could he be? He simply remembered seeing her smiling and holding up the key. They had both snuck into the cellar then. That's where they had ... well, they had kissed, that much he remembered. How could he have been so stupid? When had she put whatever drug it was into his drink? They had both been present at the opening of each bottle. He was sure of that. And yes, there had been three. It was on the third bottle, but how? They had been into the cellar twice. It was when they had stumbled down into the cellar the second time. Yes, going after the third bottle of wine. He felt he now owed the host and hostess an apology. He wasn't sure if they had drunk the best of the man's collection, but it had been very good wine. So how had she done it? How had she gotten to him? He remembered distinctly kissing her. Her laughter, them stumbling into each other. It was after the kiss that the third bottle was opened. Or was there a fourth?

God his head hurt. He leaned over, his face in his hands, his fingers dug into his forehead, massaging it. He had to think...

Yes, yes. He remembered her dancing around in the narrow cellar aisle. It wasn't a huge cellar, somewhat confining. Had they had sex? Perhaps. In any case, she had been dancing around provocatively. She had pulled the bottle from his hand and said something. He could see her clearly now, as she danced in the dim light of the ensconced candle. "Watch this," she had said. She pulled the cork out of the bottle with her teeth. They were both fairly intoxicated at this point. She was obviously a wom-

A challenge

an who wasn't concerned about her reputation. He smiled to himself at the thought. Twice he had refrained from mentioning her reputation. He had almost said it. She had in fact told him that his reputation preceded him. The first time she had said it was just after she had asked him what battles he had witnessed . . . She had asked him this with a smirk and then immediately apologized, telling him that she had known that his title was only honorary, the same as she had known that the title was 'Colonel' and not 'General.' She apologized then for having been trying to goad him. It was then that he almost said that her reputation had preceded her. He had felt that this would be stepping over a line. He could not bring himself to say such a thing to a woman. It had been true, however. Her reputation had preceded her. He had been well aware of it. He should have been more careful. How? Damn it, how had she gotten the drug into his body. Yes, she had pulled the cork with her teeth. Had he in fact already loosened it? Of course, he must have. Or had she been down in the cellar and tampered with the very bottle earlier in the evening, perhaps after the second bottle? It couldn't have been before then, and she hadn't left his sight. In fact, he had picked the bottle. So, no, that couldn't have been it. He had indeed loosened the cork, and then she pulled it out with her teeth.

At that point she pulled it from her mouth and started to lean in toward him for a kiss. He remembered this much. But how? Oh, she had stopped and placed the thing back into her mouth, holding it in her teeth. She leaned in to him, and he had opened his mouth to grab it with his teeth. He had in fact grabbed it in his teeth and pulled it from her mouth. He had then spit it onto the cellar floor and kissed her. Had she still held the outer, dry end in her teeth before passing it to him? She must have. And yes, she had taken it in her hand prior to putting it back in her mouth. Had she somehow applied the drug with her fingers to the moist end of the cork? It would have been ingenious. Well, no. This is ridiculous. He shouldn't even be wasting time worrying about such things. A simple test of the cork would perhaps indicate whether she had done it then. The cork must still be lying on the cellar floor. And the rim of the bottle could also be tested.

A challenge

This line of thinking was crazy, however, and mattered not in the least. He had gotten the better of her in the long run. She had stolen exactly what he had wanted her to steal. She would soon have been caught with the documents in her possession. He had made sure of it.

The colonel lay back on the swing. He just needed a moment or two longer, just to rest. He turned his head away from the sun. Soon he was having other visions, thoughts he remembered. He could see her clearly, dancing in the dim light of the cellar, the cork pulled from the bottle. When she raised up to face him, however, she was no more than a skeleton. The skull moved from side to side, the prominent grin. Her dark eyes danced and then receded into the skull, disappearing completely. The skull continued its side to side movement, the grin still prominent; A grin that couldn't be helped. She, or it, leaned in to kiss him then, the smell of damp earth mixed with sex, her scent, and the scent of the wine, the sweet, strong, pungent odor of poison, death lingering . . .

He was shaking, no, he was being shaken. Someone was trying to wake him. "Sir, sir . . . wake up . . . sir, we lost her."

"What?" Just as he said this, he felt he had to lunge for the porch railing. He pushed the soldier aside and vomited violently over onto the ground.

"Are you okay, sir?" The soldier was the same man who brought the paperwork to him last night.

The colonel started to look around, but then let loose again. His stomach churned and heaved. He didn't know how to answer the man's question. He started to tell him to go get a doctor. But then no, he felt better, just for a second. He then heard someone else walk up from behind. This person exited from the house. He turned enough to see the hostess from the night before. She was holding something.

"We lost her sir," the soldier was saying again.

"Shut up," the Colonel wanted to say. He didn't want the man divulging anything in front of the woman. He stood up and wiped his sleeve across his mouth.

Both men looked to the woman. She was holding something out toward the Colonel. He knew immediately what it was. "Laura said to give you these,

A challenge

she said they looked important. She said she found them on the cellar steps when she went to 'clean up'? I don't understand what she meant, but she said they looked important and she thought that they had to be yours.

The Colonel understood completely. It meant that there would be no cork, no evidence. "Anything else?" he asked.

"No, but she did apologize for having broken a bottle of wine in the cellar. I assume that's what she meant about cleaning up."

The Colonel looked at her.

"Oh, and she explained how the two of you had sat out here most of the night, talking, until, of course, you had fallen asleep. She said you were a fascinating man, more fascinating than she had anticipated . . . and, well, I'm not sure I should have mentioned that, forgive me. She did say she looked forward to seeing you again."

"Thank you," the Colonel responded.

He nodded toward the soldier and said they should be going. The two of them started away.

"Oh, your paperwork," the woman said. She held it out as the soldier ran back to retrieve it.

The Colonel continued walking. The soldier had to scramble to catch up to him. The Colonel was muttering something.

"What sir?"

"Useless," the Colonel repeated.

The soldier looked puzzled.

"The paperwork is useless . . . fake . . . fake orders, a fake map. . . Well, the map is real, but the indications of troop movements are false."

"Oh."

"So, where and how did you lose her?" As he asked this, the Colonel suddenly stopped and bent over. He thought he might have to vomit again.

"Should I get a doctor, sir?"

"No, I'll see one soon enough." He paused, still bent over. "Where did you lose her?"

"She went into an address on K street, sir, about 3:05 this morning." The soldier dug a scrap of paper out of his pocket and read off the address.

The Colonel looked up, interested once again. The address was that of a known forger. She must have had a copy made and then returned to the

A challenge

house to give the original fakes to the hostess. It would have been simple enough, could have been done in a matter of minutes. The forger wouldn't have even had to copy the map, just note the coordinates. The route could be traced on any original map of the area. He smiled and stood up. So she had bought it after all. Perhaps she hadn't been quite the challenge he had thought. Other than near poisoning him, and he would certainly be dead by now if that had been her true intent, she hadn't been that difficult to deceive.

"And then what? So that's when you lost her?"

"Why no sir. We lost her at General – s house."

"You what?" The Colonel stopped again. He felt sick again, but not from what she had given him.

"Well, she went in the front door, sir, and never exited the house. A man waited. The General emerged early this morning alone, just before sunrise."

The soldier looked harried. The Colonel realized that the man hadn't slept all night. He had a sicker feeling in the pit of his stomach though. "C'mon," he said. "We have to hurry and try to stop the General . . ."

"But he's already left, sir. Him and the troops rode off this morning."

The Colonel didn't have to ask the direction they had taken. They had taken the fake orders and fake map made up by the forger, the copies of the fakes that he had designed to deceive her. Laura Foster had somehow planted them on the General. He didn't know how, and he didn't care. Somehow, she had gotten them switched with the real ones and then returned the original fakes to the hostess to be given back to him. She had gotten the better of him. He thought of the meeting earlier in the afternoon of the day before. He could picture the General, a bombastic sort, the sort who was vain enough not to bring glasses to a meeting. In his mind's eye he saw the bumbling General shove the orders into his pocket without so much as a glance.

"He's riding into a trap," the Colonel said. "We have to stop him." All kinds of horrific visions filled his mind, a mass slaughter. It would be all his fault.

A challenge

As it turned out, however, the General and the troops did not ride into a trap. They followed the false orders and maps, but no one was there to meet them. No enemy had formed, or materialized. They had met with no resistance whatsoever. After a time, someone caught up with them and explained the situation to the General. And he simply turned around and followed the correct course.

So, what had happened? Had Laura Foster not had time to get the information to the other side? That was unlikely. She was probably sending a message to Colonel Sam Rutledge, letting him know that she was in total control. She was letting him know that she had every opportunity to deceive him, and had in fact done so, just not to the point that lives were lost. Why? Lives had been lost before. Lives had been lost by information she had passed on to the enemy. So, what was different?

Had she taken a liking to the Colonel? Had she taken pity on him? What? Somehow, he knew he would see her again. Next time, he would be better prepared. Next time . . .

The Colonel stood in the Willard hotel, drink in hand. He brought the glass to his lips only to realize it was empty. It was his third. He had been there every night for the past two weeks. Laura Foster had haunted his dreams every night for the past two weeks also. She would be the skeleton in the cellar, dancing toward him, head moving from side to side. The dream had variations in it though. Sometimes the cork would sprout plants, flowers, weeds out of its end, growing outward toward his face like tentacles. The weeds would cover his mouth, suffocating him. Other times the cork would turn into a snake and it would wrap itself around his neck, its tongue flicking out and upward as it did so. The snake would tighten its grasp and drag him up the cellar stairs. He would be trying to struggle against it as it dragged him. He would see Laura, across the room talking with the hostess. She would have the bottle of wine and the glasses in her hand. The two women would turn and look in his direction, questioning glances on each of their faces. "What could possibly be wrong?" these glances said. And then each woman's flesh would fall away, almost as if melting off of their bodies. They would be just two skeletons look-

A challenge

ing at him, mouths open. They would turn back to one another again, chattering away. And then he would be left standing in the middle of the floor.

No snake. Just him reaching out to the messenger, the soldier delivering the fake documents, only the soldier would be moving backwards as he reached for the paperwork. It would remain out of his reach as the two floated toward the door. All of the dreams were nonsense really. She had gotten the best of him, of course. And yes, her reputation had preceded her. "Next time," he muttered to himself as he placed the empty glass back onto the counter. She would not get the better of him then. They would meet again. Yes, she would be a challenge, a most difficult one, but he knew what to expect now. He would be ready. At this thought he could hear her laughter, see her dancing in the dim light of the cellar, her dark hair now fallen around her shoulders, her dark eyes flashing, the cork wedged between her teeth.

Of Mice and Men

There is a slight graying of the light. Morning, almost here. I feel the tug, just a light, barely perceptible pull. Weakness. I have to – I have to relate what is in my mind, at least a certain part of it. It is essential that I tell it, that I remain focused on the story and not on what is about to happen. What I'm going to tell you may seem horrific and yet, to me, and to those around me, they were halcyon times. Much brighter, much cheerier; though, as you will see there would normally be nothing the least bit cheerful about them.

I am a prisoner in the war of rebellion. I believe most of my enemy would call it the "war of secession." It is a war that has lasted for several years now, a war seemingly with no end in sight. I seriously doubt I will witness the end. Me and my compatriots in this prison, none of us will see the end of this war.

I call it a prison, though it is not much more than a hole dug into the side of a small mountain, nothing more than a cave really, a cave with bars on the front. I can't even tell you where it is exactly. I don't believe many know of its existence.

To keep focused on what I must I will continue:

And what were those halcyon days of which I speak? Well, they were days when we were just plain starving, a little it seems now, just a very little. The pangs of starvation then, seem mild now. Then there were still scraps. We were actually served by our enemy then. Our enemy was just a small group of fellows, not too unlike ourselves, all about the same age as us. Well, I am a bit older than the rest, in fact. A good ten years or so older. But they were somewhat like us in temperament, reasons for being in the war, etc. None of which seems to matter much now . . .

There is another tug, a slight, weak tug, pulling at what is left of the tattered threads, which I once referred to as my clothing.

Focus. I must focus on the story, not on what is happening. I cannot allow myself to be distracted. That would be insanity.

So, anyway, the halcyon times. I have to smile as I think of them. I think of my friend, well, both of my friends since I have been in captivity. I cannot think of anything prior to being taken prisoner. Those thoughts are far too fanciful, something which seems no more than what might be wrought by the imagination. It hardly seems as though they could have existed. Home? What was that? The only home I have is where I am. This is the only home I have. And the earlier times, those "halcyon days" to which I am referring, are the early days after my capture. The days when food was plentiful. Those days which shine so brightly now in my mind. Those days when we were fed almost every day, or at least once every other day. Oh, it might have been just a small scrap of potato skin, or perhaps a tiny crust of bread if we were lucky. And there might have even been a slight drop of cornmeal of sorts. Nothing fanciful you understand, but something that is beyond reach now. My mouth would produce saliva at the mere thought if I could muster up some. My mouth is dry now, however, and so too are my bones. If I were to roll over, if I had the strength . . . well it seems there would be a clattering sound of my bones clacking together. I can only imagine the organs within my thin layer of skin as drying and withering bits of something very much akin to leather drying in the sun. There is no sun, however – well, not true, of course, as I have just mentioned the slight graying of what little bit of sky I can see.

And so there were scraps. And there was even a slight trickle of water down the back side of the cave after a good hard rain. We would take turns licking the wall. Yes, how pathetic it must seem, and yet to us, to all fifty-six of us then, it was a joyous occasion.

Well, I am jumping ahead a little . . .

And again, there is a tug at my tatters. I know there are more, but I only picture one large, slowly-moving claw rising up in the darkness, the darkness that is lighting up ever so slightly into the gray of dawn. It is a dawn I am probably not destined to see in its entirety.

Does this thought frighten me. Absolutely. And so, I must steer my thoughts away from it . . .

The halcyon days. And the nights, or at least the early part of the evening, before the sleep, before the dreams of food, the nightmares. In those early evenings there would be a fire in the camp. It was a good distance away from the mouth of the cave, but with a little imagination we could see it. We actually could see the dim glow of it in the distance. We could hear the ruckus of the men. We could hear the laughter and the calling of bluffs over cards, the cursing . . . and then Lawrence would come sauntering up to the mouth of the cave and whisper in to me. Back then I could still get about. I could still stand and make my way to the entrance to meet my friend. We had struck up a bond, he and I, and discovered a mutual love of chess. It all started in fun. Lawrence of course started with *pawn to king four* and I responded in kind with black pawn to Q4 and then, the next night when he brought the scraps, he retaliated with another move, which was of course QKn to --- well, you get the picture. It really started in jest and then just continued along a more serious vein. And then when that game was finished, we started anew. It passed the time and brought us into the circle of friendship.

We were enemies, of course, but the war was too large for us to really dwell on. We each chose to ignore it for the time being. It would take its own course, resolve itself in some way. We, in effect, were no more than chess pieces that had been removed from the board, mere pawns in a much larger game. And so, the days continued on . . . and then the months . . .

And another friend showed up. Scampered would be the proper word I guess, for that is what he did, right up what only exists in my memory. And what is this? You ask. My pants leg. It is something that is no more. Oh, perhaps, if one counts threads and names them. How many threads have to be bound together to form a small bit of cloth, something that might be defined as a pant leg, or a sleeve?

Another tug, and a scratching sound in the distance. A scratching sound that might be the hind legs and cloven-hoof of the devil himself. . .

If I could muster enough energy, a chill would course through what is left of my being.

Let me again master my thoughts and steer them away from all fear. Let me return to thoughts of my new friend.

And so, my new little friend scampered up my leg and was trapped. Before he turned around to scamper back out I had him pinned. Back then, naturally, I did think of eating him, but changed my mind. I instead saved a scrap or two and began feeding him. I then let him go. Three nights later he returned. In the meantime, I had saved some more scraps and fed him again. I hadn't mentioned this to anyone at the time. By then there were only thirty-two of us, down from the fifty-six from when I was first captured.

Weeks went by and the chess games with Lawrence continued, and my other friend – Aristotle -- that's what I called him though I have no memory as to why, continued to visit. The time passed slowly, but wasn't totally unpleasant. And the war continued on about its business.

And the war ventured close. So close did it venture, in fact, that the food supply was cut totally off. It was cut off at a distance and – Ouch. I feel the scrape of a nail. Damn. It is too close, far too close. The nasty beast.

And so, the food, yes, the food ran out. By this time there were only eleven of us. Most of the initial members of my select group (and here I jest—about the select group, I mean, as though we were some fanciful men's club) died off from disease. The rest of us survived, only to starve.

And another month passed . . .

It was only after much thought and gut-wrenching guilt, that I decided to eat Aristotle. It would have been much later, however, had the others, and by now we were only seven, not been eyeing him with great gusto. A couple of the others had acquired similar delicacies and devoured them right off. I feared for Aristotle. Better, I thought, to be eaten by a friend than by a friend of a friend.

And those of our opposites on the outside didn't fare much better. They were free, of course, to wander off. They could search for fowl, but then it too must have dried up. In any case, things have since gotten so bad that there are only a few of our captors left on the outside, and they have ceased to be bothered with what becomes of those of us in the cave. There was the sound of gunfire in the distance three days ago. I believe that was what it was, but it is hard to keep track. Perhaps it was a week, or even a month past. I feel delirium set in from time to time and I lose track of thoughts along with the time. Perhaps I doze some. But dozing is a dangerous thing, for the beast seems to move quicker then. The beast, hah. Yes, there is a pause. The beast is also weak. The first initial prick, and I feel no more. Or is it already gnawing on me and I simply cannot feel it. My lower half is totally numb. And the beast, well . . .

You know, the irony of it all is that it rained a day or so ago, and there should have been water running down the back of the cave wall. I don't know. Perhaps one of the four of us left had made it to the water . . . Not I, however.

I hear a whispering sound. My name, yes, my name! The voice is Lawrence. I look over to the entrance. I cannot raise myself up, but my eyes are still functional. I can just barely see his face. He is pressed inward. There is a certain amount of excitement in his voice.

"Jacob," he calls again. "The war is over. Lee has surrendered. It's all over."

There is a pause as though he is waiting for me to respond. I would if I could. A slight wisp of breath is all that I can manage.

"Jac--" he starts again. He pauses again. "There are only two of us left, me and another. He is out looking for food, but the Blue—I mean your side has hollered that it's all over. They say we can come peacefully and --.

I think of it. There are four of us, perhaps only three. We have won. Here in the cave, on this particular battlefield we have won the war of attrition. I want to smile and yell back at Lawrence.

There is another voice, a sibilant challenge to Lawrence . . .

"Like hell," the voice says. "I ain't surrenderin' to nobody!"

Of Mice and Men

In the grayness I see Lawrence's body rise up, his face pressed against the bars. A spray of what I would imagine to be blood spews forth in a mist from his mouth as he starts to say something. I realize the dawn is rising, the light is growing even stronger. His fellow soldier has returned. He has probably bayoneted or simply stabbed Lawrence in the back with a knife, or perhaps he has slit his throat. I cannot tell. I have no strength to rise up. There is the question of whether the fellow soldiers will arrive in time. It isn't Lawrence's compatriot that I fear. No, not at all.

There had been a slight pause in the movement of the claw of the beast, or should I say, claws. I still picture it to be one large beast, which comes in the night and devours its prey. It comes under the cover of darkness. Perhaps guilt causes it to recede in the daylight, or perhaps it is simply weakness. I really should confess, however, that this "beast" to which I keep referring is no more than my fellow prisoners. This amorphous thing which comes in the night and preys on the weaker of us. I was once a part of the thing, but now it is made up of the two or three of us left. It is very weak, and so the tugs, the slow movement, ever so slight, as the thing, things, or should I say fellow beings – the stronger, comes and devours the weaker. It is really just a question of survival. Now that the motion has started it will not cease. No soldier will arrive in time to free us. The thing is of one mind now. It only knows survival – devour the weakest of the group for sustenance. I am the weakest. Perhaps if I had somehow saved Aristotle until later. Perhaps then I would have survived. Maybe I was too greedy, too glutinous. Would it be better, though, to be a part of the thing? I was a part of it before without any thought. But now – now, when a chance of rescue is close. Perhaps. . .

There is still a pause, a silence. I start to glance over. No. No I can't. It is enough that I see it in my mind's eye. I see the thing. I only imagine that I have glanced at it. But no, I must. I must look. I move my eyes to my side. I see four eyes. So, there are only two of us left, not counting myself, of course. The eyes are glazed. The hunger of the beast is all that is left. The thing is emaciated, horrific looking. Lips are peeled back, teeth prominent in a grin of delight. A meal, a chance to survive. I see the glow in the four glazed eyes. The glow of hunger is stronger than the dawn. A part of the thing disappears, and the tugs begin again. Only two eyes remain looking at me. There is no sympathy, nothing. Only cold, stark hunger. The tugs are much stronger now, more insistent. The claws rip and tear now, the thing seems down-right frantic. The second pair of eyes disappear. There seems to be a growling, almost a battle, and then mewling sound, or am I imagining that. Then there is a frenzied ripping. I can only be imagining it, however, for I am beyond feeling. I don't know whether it is fabric that is being torn into, or flesh. I can't believe there is much in the way of either left to provide much sustenance. The ripping continues, the beast grows mildly stronger. It rests temporarily out of exhaustion. The ripping stops, only to start in again a few minutes later. I am numb to it, sort of. There is pain, but it is too excruciating to even consider. I think of Lawrence, the spray of blood, a mist, floating in the grayness of the dawn. How close is his body to the bars at the mouth of the cave? I think of how much more of a meal he would be, and try to will the beast devouring me to think of the same. There might, after all, be an arm or leg just close enough. The ripping stops. I see first two eyes look at me, then the other two appear. They both disappear. Is it the dawn that gives the beast pause? Probably not, not anymore. . . It is more apt to be that the beast, the two that are left had the same thought that I just had. Perhaps Lawrence is close enough. A meaty arm or leg, much more enticing of a meal than my mere skin and bone. I doubt that I have enough flesh left to amount to anything, even anything the size of my former mouse friend Aristotle. Perhaps one of the two will perish from exhaustion on the way to the mouth of the cave. Then the thing will be smaller. Just two eyes then . . . The beast is also starving. How much energy will it have to expend to get to the mouth of the cave, to reach Lawrence? I again feel a tug. The same thought must have occurred to the beast. And another thought also – that perhaps there is enough meat on my bones to provide just enough sustenance so that the beast can make it to the better meal . . .

Acknowledgments

I'd like to thank Caroline Barnhill for the fine editing job. Any mistakes still in the book are solely mine. Probably due to my continually tweaking sentences here and there – after she has finished her job!

Made in the USA
Lexington, KY
04 November 2019